WANDERERS

John Wyndham was born in 1903. Until 1911
he lived in Edgbaston, Birmingham, and then
in many parts of England. After a wide
experience of the English preparatory school
he was at Bedales from 1918 to 1921. Careers
he tried included farming, law, commercial art,
and advertising, and he first started writing
short stories, intended for sale, in 1925. From
1930 to 1939 he wrote stories of various kinds
under different names, almost exclusively for
American science fiction publications. He also
wrote detective novels. During the war he was
in the Civil Service and afterwards in the Army.
In 1946 he went back to writing. His most
famous novels are THE DAY OF THE
TRIFFIDS, THE KRAKEN WAKES (both of
which have been translated into several
languages), THE MIDWICH CUCKOOS
(filmed as THE VILLAGE OF THE DAMNED)
and TROUBLE WITH LICHEN. John Wyndham
died in March 1969.

Wanderers of Time

John Wyndham

Writing as John Beynon Harris
Introduction by Walter Gillings

NEW ENGLISH LIBRARY
Hodder and Stoughton

The characters and situations in this book are entirely imaginary and bear no relation to any real person or actual happening.

This book is sold subject to the condition that it shall not, by way of trade or otherwise, be lent, re-sold, hired out or otherwise circulated without the publisher's prior consent in any form of binding or cover other than that in which it is published and without a similar condition including this condition being imposed on the subsequent purchaser.

No part of this publication may be reproduced or transmitted in any form or by any means, electronically or mechanically, including photocopying, recording or any information storage or retrieval system, without either the prior permission in writing from the publisher or a licence, permitting restricted copying, issued by the Copyright Licensing Agency, 33–34 Alfred Place, London WC1E 7DP.

Printed and bound in Great Britain for Hodder and Stoughton Paperbacks, a division of Hodder and Stoughton Ltd., Mill Road, Dunton Green, Sevenoaks, Kent, TN13 2YA. (Editorial Office: 47 Bedford Square, London WC1B 3DP) by Richard Clay Ltd, Bungay, Suffolk.

ISBN 0-450-42015-9

Contents

BEFORE THE TRIFFIDS...

To those who have enjoyed *The Day of the Triffids*, *The Kraken Wakes* and other John Wyndham novels, it may come as a surprise to know that he was writing imaginative fiction with conspicuous success forty years ago. His novels, *The Secret People* and *Stowaway to Mars* (both recently republished by Coronet Books), delighted tens of thousands of readers when they first appeared in the 1930s as serial stories in a popular weekly as well as in volume form. Most of his shorter stories, however, first appeared in a magazine specialising in 'science fiction' (a term he detested) which was published in the U.S.A., which offered the only receptive market for most of his work in this *genre*. Writing under his own name, John Beynon Harris became familiar to readers of *Wonder Stories* as a contributor of thoroughly convincing tales in which the motivating idea, however fantastic, was always subservient to the narrative and the characters as believable as the background, however exotic.

Not until 1937, when the British magazine *Tales of Wonder* began to cultivate this restricted field, were more than a few hundred readers on this side of the Atlantic able to enjoy such stories as you will find in this volume. And soon afterwards came *Fantasy*, to widen still further the international circle of admirers who knew him equally well as John Beynon.

In the days before the world had heard of Wernher von Braun or Konstantin Tsiolkovsky, the concept of space-travel was derided by all but the readers and writers of science fiction. To John Beynon the notion was part of his stock-in-trade, which he replenished by listening to the debates of the British Interplanetary Society, then a mere handful of enthusiasts. In 'The Last Lunarians,' with its visions of lunar diggings, he anticipated today's Moonwalk activities with an accuracy which would seem uncanny if we did not know how well he did his research—among speculations as well as facts. Hopefully, the disastrous turn of events in 'Derelict of Space' will be avoided; but the idea of salvaging vessels which have come to grief in the interplanetary void is not inconsistent with recent orbital crises which have kept the whole world in suspense.

The mythical kingdom of 'Spheres of Hell' might seem, now, even more remote. Yet the irony is still to be relished, and I have been tempted to include it here because, for sheer artistry combined with originality, it has always appealed to me as among the finest examples of John Beynon's work. In 'Child of Power,' for which he used the pseudonym Wyndham Parkes (derived from two of his middle names), those who are familiar with *The Midwich Cuckoos* may recognise a near-relative of those remarkable children. But perhaps the most startling of all his creations are the insectile machines you will encounter in 'Wanderers of Time,' one of his more ambitious tales which takes us into the future to a time when man is no longer the dominant creature on this planet. Here is a story which will never cease to evoke the essential quality of wonder which is the basis of all good science fiction.

Ilford, Essex

WALTER GILLINGS
May 1972

WANDERERS OF TIME

CHAPTER ONE

THE TIME-TRAVELLER

THE pompous little man who had been strutting his way through a wood near the Saber property, a few miles out of Chicago, came suddenly to a standstill, blinked rapidly and dropped his lower jaw. For perhaps five seconds he stared before him with a fish-like expression of astonishment; then a fear of the inexplicable, inherited from far-off ancestors, sent him scuttling for cover. Once in the safe obscurity of the bushes, he turned again to goggle amazedly at the centre of the glade.

A moment before, he had faced a small clearing holding in itself nothing more substantial than golden sunlight. Then, even as he looked—he was certain he had neither blinked nor turned his head—a glittering cylinder had appeared; and it stayed there, in the exact centre of the open space. looking like an immense projectile of polished steel—an apparition sudden and alarming enough to make the little man entirely justified in running. Now, from his vantage-point, he examined it with less panic and a rising indignation. The cylinder's length he estimated at somewhere about eighteen feet, and its diameter at three feet The metal covering appeared at this range to be seamless, and it scintillated in the afternoon sunshine with a harsh brightness.

'Not quite like steel,' he corrected himself. 'Colder ... more like chromium plate. But what the devil is it?'

The discretion of remaining among the bushes appealed to him far more than the valour of a closer inspection. A large object like this, which could appear abruptly and in complete silence before one's very nose, was to be treated with circumspection. Less than half a minute later, he snatched a sudden breath. A rectangular patch of darkness had become visible in the upper surface of the cylinder. Fascinatedly, he watched the slit broaden as a panel was slid back. A man's head was thrust cautiously through the opening, turning to left and right as he reconnoitred. Presently, seemingly satisfied that he was un-observed, he slid the panel back to its limit and levered himself out of the opening.

A glance at the man's full face brought a short gasp from the watcher, and he moved involuntarily, snapping a twig beneath his foot. For a moment he held his breath, but became easier when the other showed no sign of having heard the sharp crack. He had turned back to his machine—for such it seemed to be—and with one arm plunged into the dark interior, was fumbling for something. When he straightened again, the little man stiffened, for the right hand held a ponderous revolver which pointed in his direction. Any hope that this might be accidental was quickly dispersed.

'Come on,' commanded the man in the glade. 'Out of that, quick!'

He flourished his weapon impatiently at the watcher's momentary hesitation. 'Put 'em up, and come out,' he repeated.

The man in the bushes waited no longer. Hands well above his head, he marched into the open.

'Who are you?' asked the other.

'Henry Q. Jones,' the little man answered. He was finding himself less afraid of the man before him than he had been of the impersonal cylinder. He even added: 'Who are you, if it comes to that?'

'My name is no business of yours,' replied the other, watching him closely, 'but it happens to be Roy Saber.'

Henry Q. Jones' mouth started to open, and then shut quickly.

'You don't believe me?'

Henry Q. grunted non-commitally.

'Why not?'

'Well, if you must know, for one thing, Roy Saber is younger than you are—though you're mighty like him—and, another thing, I happened to see Roy Saber board the Chicago train a couple of hours ago.'

'Awkward,' commented the other. 'Nevertheless, I *am* Roy Saber.' He contemplated his captive for a moment.

Henry Q. Jones returned the scrutiny with curiosity. The other's clothes differed greatly from the little man's propriety of dress. His suit was of an unusually bright blue, and though the trousers were full in cut, the jacket fitted closely; and though it gave a double-breasted effect, the front flap was in reality carried right across to the left side and secured by a zip-fastener. The broad lapel was of a slightly lighter shade of blue and stretched, like a triangular slash, from the right shoulder to its apex on the left of the waist. The neck-opening showed a soft collar with surprisingly long points, and a tie striped with the two blues of the suit.

'Well, Henry Q.,' he said at length. 'I've nothing against you personally except that you are a damned nuisance, but I'll have to tie you up or you might ditch the whole plan.'

Roy Saber was inexpert at trussing. He used more rope than was necessary, and his knots were the jumbles of the amateur; nevertheless, he contrived to reduce the other to a state of log-like immobility. Then he produced a handkerchief and carefully began to roll it diagonally.

'I'm sorry, but I can't afford to have you bawling for help. Open!'

Henry Q.'s mouth remained obstinately shut. He received a painful jab in the ribs.

'Open!'

He opened. His captor turned back to the cylinder and carefully shut the entrance-panel. Then he thrust the big revolver into a pocket, and picked up the bound man. At the edge of the clearing, he laid him down among the concealing bushes.

'I'll only be about a couple of hours,' he remarked considerately.

Henry Q. twisted his head and glared balefully after him as he disappeared between the tree-trunks.

Roy Saber was back in something under the two hours, and he did not return alone. By his side walked a girl, whose fair hair shimmered in the shafts of sunlight which penetrated the foliage. Her face was fresh-coloured and her chin was rounded, but firm. With her blue eyes and impertinent nose, none could deny her prettiness; but somehow her mouth, though not too small, failed to suggest an equable disposition. She looked up at her companion with a slightly puzzled frown.

'But, Roy,' she said, 'you look older. Your hair's not all black —I'm sure I can see grey streaks here and there. And you're wearing such funny clothes. What's happened?'

'I *am* older, Betty, but there's no time to explain just now. You must wait a bit.'

He looked admiringly at her, so neat and lithe in her close-fitting red frock—a deep red, to contrast with her fairness. They paused beside the clump of bushes where he had hidden Henry Q. As he parted the leaves, Betty heard him mutter under his breath.

'What is it?'

Roy did not answer for a moment. He stared thoughtfully at a few tangled cords which were the only evidence of Henry

Q.'s late presence. Then he glanced out at the clearing where the cylinder still lay.

'Wait a minute,' he directed, and ran off to one side. He was back in less than the minute. 'It's all right,' he said, leading her into the open. 'I thought someone might be laying for me behind the machine.'

He thought for a moment. 'I meant to talk to you a bit before we risked anything, but this changes things. We'll have to hurry.'

'I don't understand—what are you talking about?'

'I'll explain it all later,' he said, as he hastened her towards the cylinder. He drew the revolver from his pocket, and she looked at it askance.

'What——?'

'Later,' he repeated, hurriedly sliding back two panels in the curved surface. He pointed to the end space. 'In you get, Betty!'

She peered doubtfully at the dark opening. It was possible to see that the whole of the interior was thickly padded and supplied with loose cushions.

'But——'

'Quick, quick!' he insisted, lifting and helping her through the space. He slid the cover over her. Even as it clicked into place, he heard a crackle of running feet among the trees and a voice came bellowing across the clearing.

'Stop where you are! Put 'em up!'

Henry Q. Jones had evidently returned, with reinforcements. With eel-like agility, Roy slid into the cylinder. As he did so, two men in uniform burst from the trees and came pelting into the clearing, pistols in hand.

'He's got a gun,' called Henry Q.'s voice from somewhere behind them.

Roy had a glimpse of one of the policemen taking aim. Like lightning, he ducked and slammed the panel over his head. There came a crash as the bullet struck the cylinder somewhere forward of him. He blanched at the thought of the blob of lead in its delicate machinery, but thanked the Lord it had hit the forward compartment and not the rear, where Betty lay. In frenzied haste, he twisted the dials on his small control-panel, and snapped in the minor switches.

The policemen had reached the cylinder now. They were battering on it with their pistol-butts, and Roy could hear their voices raised in a muffled shouting. With a desperate hope that the shot had injured no vital part, he wrenched over the main switch.

Outside two bewildered policemen stared open-mouthed at each other. Even while they hammered on its walls, the cylinder had vanished without trace.

'Well I'll be——!' one muttered. The other said nothing; he looked badly scared. Henry Q. Jones emerged from the safety of the trees.

'And you call yourselves cops,' he sneered, unpleasantly.

Roy's biggest surprise, when he had made his first journey in the cylindrical machine, had been the entire absence of sensation. He had closed the sliding lid and shut out the view of his workroom. Then he had pulled the switch and waited, tensely, for something to happen. Apparently nothing did, and he had started to reopen the panel with the conviction that the experiment had miscarried and that further adjustment would be necessary. He had gasped to find that, after all, the contrivance had worked perfectly—had, in fact, moved him back ten years in time, without changing his position on Earth.

It was the more surprising in the face of the witnesses' prophecy of utter failure. Sam Hanson, his attorney, had protested:

'It's ridiculous, Roy—impossible! Why, if you did go back ten years, you would have to be in two places at one and the same time—you might even meet yourself! It would be entire confusion. Just think of the disorganisation that success would imply. There'd be neither past nor future any more.'

Roy had shook his head. 'I shan't meet my younger self: I should remember it now, if that meeting had ever occurred. And as for being in two places at the same time—well, why not? Has anyone ever proved it impossible? It is just a ridiculous assertion made by persons completely ignorant of the nature of time. Anyway, I'm going to try!'

And he had succeeded. Succeeded, not only in travelling through time, but also in his main purpose, which was the finding of Betty. Now he was carrying her home in triumph. He had meant to put the plan before her first, but the intrusion of Henry Q. Jones had upset that. It would be good to see the amazed faces in his work-room when they both climbed out of the machine....

For a second after he had pulled the switch, nothing happened. Then there came a jolt. The cylinder swayed, as though poised uncertainly. Further and further over it leaned, until it tilted violently over to the right, rolling him up the padded side of his compartment. As it twisted, he wondered what could have happened; after that, he became too busy to speculate. The cylinder was bumping unevenly, and turning with increasing speed. Grimly, he drove his elbows and knees into the padding, in an effort to wedge his body instead of having it bounced around like a ball. The forward end brought up against some obstruction with a crash; the machine slewed violently, and the bump with which Roy's head met the end of the compartment was but little softened by the padding.

He thought with anguish of the havoc that crash must have caused amid the mechanism. He stretched one hand up towards the sliding panel. The movement, small as it was, served to upset the precarious balance. Again the cylinder canted over, and recommenced its jolting progress, spinning and bouncing like a runaway barrel as it went. After long-drawn minutes, it slowed and rolled jerkily to a stop. Roy moved cautiously to assure himself that, this time, it was stable. It was, but he made a disconcerting discovery.

'Betty!' he shouted.

'Yes?' Her voice came faintly through the partition between their compartments.

'Are you all right?'

The reply was unintelligible.

'We're upside down,' he continued, 'and I can't open the panel. When I call three, throw yourself against the right side, and we may be able to roll on half a turn.' He paused, then: 'One—two—*three*.'

The cylinder lurched a little, hovered, and then settled back.

'Try again.'

The second attempt met with no more success than the first. Roy wiped his brow; it was getting very warm in the cramped quarters.

'Something in the way,' he called. 'Better try swinging her from side to side, and see if we can roll over it.'

They struggled for over a minute, but very little movement was possible. There appeared to be obstructions on both sides, and Roy began to fear that his time-traveller would prove a double coffin.

'Once more,' he yelled.

Still the cylinder refused to surmount the obstacles. Roy lay back, sweating and exhausted, puzzling to find a way out of the situation. Once he thought he heard a movement outside, but decided that it must be the girl stirring.

'Betty!' he shouted again.

As though in answer, there came three deliberate taps on the outer wall.

'Betty, there's somebody outside! Let's try again. One—two —three.'

He threw every ounce of his weight against the side. Hesitantly the cylinder rolled, this time, until the ports came uppermost. For a second it hung poised; then there came a clank against the side, just in time to stop it from settling back.

CHAPTER TWO

THE MAN FROM 10,402

SWIFTLY Roy reached up and slid back his panel, to admit a welcome gust of fresh air. Sitting up, he thrust out his head and looked back, to see that Betty's panel also was open. Her dishevelled head appeared, but she gazed beyond rather than at him. He spun round, and stared in astonishment at the figure which stood by the battered forepart of the cylinder. His surprise was reciprocated, and for some seconds the two faced one another in silence.

Roy felt a shock at the sight of the man before him. He stood barely four feet in height, and his body, hands and feet were in good proportion to that size. But his totally bald head was of normal dimensions—perhaps a trifle larger—and gave an odd effect of being insecurely balanced on his small frame. His visible clothing consisted of a single silvery garment designed on the lines of a smock, but caught around his waist by a broad leather belt to which a number of dangling objects were hooked.

He approached them as they climbed out of the cylinder. Betty shrank back, an expression of disgust on her face. Roy pulled himself together.

'You speak English?' he inquired.

'English is my language,' the other replied, his accent differing but little from Roy's own. He continued to regard the two with a puzzled air.

'Then we have you to thank for our rescue. I am Roy Saber, and this lady is Miss Betty Mordan.'

'And I,' returned the little man, 'am Del Two-Forty-A.'

In the ensuing pause, Roy became aware of the unexpected aspect of the countryside. A large, red Sun was pouring down from the cloudless sky to show, not the fertile land he had left, but a tumbled scene of sand and rock. Nowhere was it relieved by a single soothing patch of green, and over all hung the deathly silence of desolation. They stood in a steep-sided valley, whose floor was dotted with fallen masses of rock and banked in many parts with drifts of sand. An unhurried river ran twisting past them, disappearing where the curve of the valley cut off their view, a mile away. There was inexpressible dreariness in the barren vista. Roy glanced up at the hillside behind them.

'It's a miracle we weren't smashed in rolling down there,' he murmured.

'It certainly is,' replied Betty's voice, harshly. 'And no credit to you, either. Now suppose you get us back—and quick. I'd like to know what sort of game you think you're playing with me?'

Roy stared at her, and then recovered himself. After all, there was some excuse for her tone.

'Something went wrong,' he began. 'That cop——'

'Oh, yes? Something went wrong, did it? Well, it's your job to see that it darned well goes right again. Say, do you realise that this is abduction?'

Roy spread his hands helplessly, looking ruefully at his ruined time-traveller.

'I can't make that work again. When the cop fired into the machinery, he jammed something. And now that roll down here's smashed the thing right up.'

The dwarf had been peering interestedly into the wreckage of the fore-part, prying among the tangled wiring and examining the remains of shattered vacuum tubes. Still looking perplexed, he turned to Roy again.

'What is your date?' he asked.

Roy suffered another surprise. He had not expected the immediate recognition of his time-traveller for what it was.

'I'm from 1951,' he replied.

'1941,' Betty corrected. 'What's wrong with your memory?'

'No, 1951. I'll explain later.'

'So early? That is remarkable,' said the little man, indicating the cylinder. 'My own date is 10,402.'

'Say, what is all this about?' Betty demanded.

'It means that the cop's shot has landed us in the year 10,402,' Roy informed her.

Betty's regard was scornful and scathing. 'Suppose,' she suggested, 'you quit the kidding. I'm in no mood for it. What's more, the sooner you get us back home, the better it's going to be for you. Get me?'

Roy stared at her. Her menacing tone of voice shocked him. He felt bewildered, as though the girl he knew had suddenly turned into a stranger. In his surprise, he had forgotten Del, who broke in as he turned:

'You are mistaken. I meant to say only that I started from the year 10,402. What this year is, I do not know—save that it is many millennia later.'

'That's right,' said Betty. 'You must keep the joke up! But I'm not laughing—I can't see that you're both so damned funny as you think you are.'

A plaintive expression passed over Del's face. 'What does she mean?' he inquired.

Roy changed the subject. Turning to the dwarf: 'Why did you come to this year?' he asked.

Del shook his head. 'Something was wrong with my machine, just as something was wrong with yours. It is over there.' He pointed to a large boulder some twenty yards away. The end of a bright metal bar protruded from behind it.

'It is smashed too?'

'Only slightly damaged.'

'Let's go and look at it.'

Before they left the cylinder, Roy groped in the control compartment and produced his revolver. He stuffed a handful of cartridges into each side pocket, and they moved off. Betty followed sulkily.

Del's machine bore no resemblance to his own. The impression it gave was of a cubical cage with six-foot sides, and built of an intricate criss-cross strutting of two metals, one silvery, the other black. A padded bucket-seat was set in the middle, with a small control-board before it. The driving mechanism was evidently contained in three black boxes clamped to the base framework and inter-connected by heavy cables. Roy's heart sank as he saw it. An idea that parts of his own cylinder might be used to render Del's machine workable was roughly quashed. The two contrivances had nothing constructionally in common.

Del mutely pointed to one base corner, where the framework was wrenched and sadly twisted. It was also noticeable that the cover of one of the black boxes was split open. Roy leaned over to examine the damage more closely.

'You see,' Del began, 'unlike your machine, this works by the capillary absorption of light. The rays striking——'

'Look, look!' cried Betty, behind them.

They wheeled to find her pointing up at the sky-line of the opposite hill, where a row of strange objects was progressing in single file. There was nothing to give them scale, and Roy was able to estimate their height only very roughly in the neighbourhood of twenty feet. Each consisted of an egg-shaped main bulk balanced upon two trellised supports, tapering towards the ground. These 'legs' were jointed in the middle and, like the 'body' above, were coloured a bright red. Around the main upper bulk, complexities of levers were folded.

For some seconds, the three stood motionless and staring. 'What——?' Roy began; but Del shook his head before the question was formed. There had been nothing like these in his century.

From the leader of the five red contrivances, a jointed arm suddenly swept to the ground and caught up a rock. Without pausing in its stride, it sent the mass, fully half a ton in weight, sailing across the valley. Somewhere on the hill behind them it landed, with a crash and a clatter of metal. Roy abruptly dragged his companions into the shadow of the nearest boulder, fearful that discovery might bring a rock hurtling in their direction.

The red machines strode on their way with unhurried, stilted gait, a faint metallic clanking accompanying their movements. Apparently the rock had accomplished its purpose, whatever that might be: at any rate, no more followed, and the metal arm was refolded against the egg-shaped body-piece. The three watched in silence as the five red figures carried themselves away in long, stiff strides. Even Betty's indignation had momentarily given way to nervousness.

'What were they?' she demanded.

Roy shrugged his shoulders. Speculation was worse than useless. He stood up to assure himself that the machines were truly out of sight. As he rose, there came a clatter of metal against stone, a sound rapidly approaching up the valley. His hand snatched at his revolver.

A group of machines came abruptly round the masking turn of the valley. Contrary to Roy's expectations, they bore little similarity to the rock-hurling monsters of the hill-top. Only the shape of the body-pieces was similar. They stood some seven feet to the highest point of the rounded back, and their egg-shaped hulls progressed with a scurrying motion upon six jointed legs. Four waving metal tentacles protruded from the extreme front and, above them, two lenses were set flush in the smooth case-work.

They stopped at sight of Roy, with the suddenness of complete surprise, and stood motionless save for their waving

tentacles. He called in a low tone to the others to remain
hidden, and stepped forward, revolver in hand. An indecisive
movement ran through the ranks of the machines. They
seemed on the point of retreat; but at that moment Betty,
ignoring Roy's advice, chose to emerge from behind the rock.

The machines moved as one, and came scuttering forward
with a great waving of tentacles. Three shots from Roy's revolver crashed among them, with no visible result. He turned,
to become aware that Del was now out of concealment, fumbling with a tube which looked like a flashlight.

'Run!' Roy snapped. 'Get to the river!'

He had some faint hope that the machines might not be
water-tight. Betty was already fleeing, and Del turned to follow her. Roy stayed long enough to send another three shots,
and then started to run with the machines almost upon him,
but he made no more than a dozen yards before something
fouled his ankle and flung him heavily to earth. As the
machines overtook him, he saw Del turn and raise his tube,
and two tentacles of the nearest pursuer fell to the ground as
though they had been chopped off. Del switched the tube at
another, but now there were a half-dozen of the machines
bearing down on him.

One more tentacle fell; then, like a silver whip-lash, another
struck the tube from the dwarf's hand and wrapped itself
around him. The tube sailed high through the air and fell
with a splash into the river. A fountain of steam, like the
jetting plume of a geyser, roared into the sky, while the water
all around broke, seething and bubbling. Betty, almost at the
brink, recoiled. The feeler of a pursuing machine snatched at
her, tearing away her red frock. It tossed the garment away,
wrapped the feeler like a shining belt about her waist, and
carried her back towards Roy and Del.

With relief, Roy saw that no injury seemed intended towards any of the party. Each of them was carefully picked up
in a wrapping of tentacles, and the machines set off down the
valley in the direction from which they had appeared. For five
miles they followed the tortuous river course; then the hills
were left behind and they came out upon a level plain where
patches of coarse grass, half choked by drifting sand, struggled
hardily to grow. The machines changed their formation as
they reached the open country, and Roy found that Del's captor was travelling alongside his own, while Betty's was some
yards in advance. He spoke across to Del, and received assurance that he was uninjured.

'The most unfortunate thing is that my tube is lost,' the

dwarf added.

'What was it? I've never seen anything like that before.'

'A heat-ray. You did not have such things in the twentieth century?'

Roy shook his head, and went on to talk about their captors. On this subject, both were equally at a loss.

'Robots? Distant-control mechanisms? They might be either,' Del suggested.

'Or, perhaps, vehicles,' added Roy. 'The bodies of the race may have atrophied into complete uselessness and made these machines necessary for carrying the brains.'

Del considered the theory an unlikely one. 'But they certainly have a high level of intelligence. No doubt you noticed that they are bringing along our wrecked machines?'

Roy, glancing back past the curving metal flank of his captor, could see his battered cylinder supported by the tentacles of two following machines.

CHAPTER THREE

CAPTIVES OF THE MACHINES

BETTY had caught the sound of their voices. She called back, querulously, to know why Roy did not do something. The indignity of capture had done nothing to soothe her temper and, now that no immediate danger threatened, her tone had resumed its nagging quality. After a devastating flow of abuse, Del inquired curiously:

'Is she hurt?'

'Yes; but not in the way you mean. She's been pinked in her pride. She was riled to begin with. Now she's lost her dress and is being carried over a desert in her underclothes. She's hurt, all right!'

Del looked surprised at Roy's tone. He was silent for some moments before he suggested:

'I wonder whether that red dress had anything to do with the attack? It was at her appearance that the machines went into action, and when the dress was torn away, they became much calmer. Also, the first machines we saw were coloured red....'

No reply came from Roy. He seemed uninterested in the suggestion. Del relapsed into a contemplative silence.

During their advance, the country was losing severity. The hard, wiry grass gradually became supplanted by a softer type, growing more luxuriantly and almost hiding the sandy soil. A dotting of infrequent, stunted shrubs managed to find sustenance. In the distance, a line of darker green suggested the presence of trees.

'Thank God for that,' Roy said, fervently. 'I had begun to fear that the world might be all desert.'

'I think we're headed for *that*,' said Del. He nodded ahead towards a vast spike which stabbed up into the heavens.

Roy looked at it. The base was hidden among the trees many miles away, but even at this distance he could tell that its height must be measured in thousands of feet. Observation at such a distance gave no clue to its nature, save that it was too isolated and too abrupt to be a natural formation; yet it was roughly shaped, lacking the symmetry and lines of a normal artificial structure. Its vastness induced a sense of importance and a feeling of fatalism, and he watched it with rising disquiet until the great, red Sun died in a livid blaze.

The machines did not hesitate, but held to their course through a mysterious, dark world in which the only sound was the scuttering of their own progress. Throughout the night they pursued a winding way among the trees, still bearing in the direction of the mighty spire. The darkness appeared to have little or no hampering effect upon them, and dawn found them with but few miles left to cover. And it was with a very weary thankfulness that the captives were carried clear of the forest into the open space surrounding the base of the artificial mountain. For they were not only fatigued, but hungry and thirsty, and oppressed by the impossibility of making their wants known.

The mass of the building at short range was stupendous and overwhelming, rearing before them like an ill-smoothed cliff and dwarfing them into a feeling of helplessness. One high, arched entrance pierced it at ground level, and through this they were borne into ever-increasing gloom.

For five minutes they travelled through pitch-black corridors filled with the scuttering sounds of many mobile machines; then their captors came to a stop, for the first time since they had left the rocky valley. There came a click, followed by a rattle, as a door of sheet metal slid up into the roof. Beyond it was revealed a dimly lit, cave-like hall. The binding tentacles loosened, to set the three on their feet. Gentle thrusts sent them staggering stiffly forward. The metal door clattered down behind them.

For a moment they stood silently gazing about them. The meagre light emanated from a group of translucent balls placed in the middle of the floor, and served to show imperfectly the rear end of the hall. Of the other end, beyond the lights, nothing could be seen but a velvety darkness. Roy took a step forward, and then stopped abruptly at the sound of something moving in the shadows. He drew his revolver and pointed it menacingly, as he continued his advance. Two figures came dimly into view, rounding the clustered light-balls.

'Stop!' Roy ordered. He turned to speak to Del, but the little man brushed him aside and rushed excitedly forward, calling to the two figures.

Roy, with Betty beside him, was left to look on wonderingly as the three greeted one another. He could see, now, that the strangers were similar to Del both in stature and clothing. A few moments later, they were led up and introduced. They regarded Roy and Betty with the same curiosity as Del had shown at the first meeting, and evinced the same incredulous surprise at hearing of their twentieth-century origin. Del explained:

'These are my friends, Kal Two Eleven A and Ril Three Thirty-Two A. They were both of them my assistants,' he added.

Roy's wonderment grew. 'Then you are also from 10,402?' he asked.

The dwarfed Kal shook his large head. 'No, we are from 10,424. It took us over twenty years to duplicate the time-travelling machine.'

'But you know what date we have reached now?'

Again Kal shook his head. 'We have no more means of discovering than you have. One can only guess——'

The clatter of the metal door cut short his speculation. The group spun round, to see three more human beings urged gently into the hall. There was a fleeting look of alarm on the face of the tallest of the newcomers. As the door rattled down behind them, he produced a black tube and advanced, holding it trained upon them.

'Who are you?' he demanded in a firm tone. 'And by what right have you made us prisoners?'

Roy looked the man over. He stood perhaps six feet, and was built with slender strength, in excellent proportions. His hair, though fine and sparse, was jet-black, as were the eyebrows which ran in a single frowning bar across his forehead. His jaw was square, his mouth thin-lipped and firm, and his eyes keen. The strength of character which he showed seemed out of accord with the soft silk (or synthetic silk) garments which clung in lustrous folds to his knees. One of his companions was similarly clad. The third newcomer hung back, little more than a shadow in the dim light.

'Who are you, I say?' repeated the speaker.

It was Del who answered. He gave particulars of his own group, and countered with a like request. The new arrival put away his tube.

'I am Hale Lorrence, and this is my companion, Julian Tyne.' He indicated the other silk-robed man. 'We have come from the year 3920.'

'And the third member of your party?'

The man who called himself Hale shrugged his shoulders. 'She has told me that her name is Jessica Tree. She claims to have started from A.D. 2200.'

The vaguely seen figure stepped forward. She revealed herself as a girl of perhaps twenty-four or twenty-five. A russet tunic, heavily worked with metallic thread, covered her to her knees. Her legs were a sunburnt brown, and her feet were encased in shoes to match her tunic. Black hair, cut short, clustered about her softly oval face, and she surveyed the company from a pair of lustrously dark eyes. Her tone, as she spoke, betrayed her dislike of Hale's manner.

'It is more than a mere claim,' she said, coldly. 'It is a fact that I come from 2200. . . . What year is this?'

Del shrugged his shoulders. 'That is what we all want to know.'

'I don't,' cried Betty's voice, viciously. 'I don't care a damn what year it is! The one thing I'm certain about is that I have been kidnapped. And if somebody doesn't do something to get me back where I belong—and do it darned quick—there's going to be trouble around here. See?'

Hale Lorrence regarded her speculatively for a moment, and then turned to Del.

'We are hungry and thirsty. Is there any food here?'

Kal had ascertained that there were dishes of water at the other end of the cavern, but no food.

After they had drunk, Roy started on an exploratory tour of their prison. He could discover no opening other than that closed by the metal door. The walls would have easily revealed any crack, for they were smooth and unornamented. The finish to them puzzled him not a little. Although they were hard and smooth, the effect was not that obtained by any mechanical finishing process. It was, he felt, the kind of result one would expect if a giant hand had attempted to shape the material in its plastic state, without the use of tools.

The end of the circuit found him no wiser than the beginning. He returned to find the rest of the party endeavouring to clear away some of their mystification. Del was saying:

'... therefore, this must be a kind of "dead" spot in time. It is as though our machines had been thrown into the flow of time and swept along until, for some unguessable reason, they met an obstruction at this point. Every one of us has arrived here because his machine was faulty in some way or other. To take an illustration—a bad one, I admit, but enough for our purpose—one may consider time as a river. You may turn boats adrift on it at many points, and they will all collect together at the same serious obstacle, whether they have travelled a hundred miles or two miles. We are now at some period where the straight flow of time has been checked—perhaps it is even turning back upon itself. We know no details at present, but it is certain that the same curious phenomenon has thrown us all together.'

'But,' Hale objected, 'time, like space, surely is curved?'

'It may be—in fact, it must be; but I see no reason why there should not be interruptions in time. After all, are not the stars interruptions in space?'

'You mean that space may interrupt time in the same way that time distorts space?'

'Roughly, yes—if you can consider the two apart, which I find impossible. I merely repeat that we have struck some barrier and been thrown up like so much jetsam.'

'Then there may be others, besides ourselves?'

'As many others as made faulty time-travellers.'

Julian Tyne joined in the conversation. He spoke with a lazy drawl which irritated his listeners.

'But what is all this?' He waved a languid arm. 'This place, these queer machines—both the tall, red things and the smaller, white ones which caught us—what are they all doing? It doesn't seem to make sense.'

Del glanced at him. 'Suppose an alien form was plunged into your world of 3920,' he said. 'How much do you suppose he would understand? I doubt whether it would "make sense" to him. In fact, I would go so far as to suggest that you would have very little understanding of the organisation of my world of 10,402, had your machine taken you there instead of here.'

Roy broke in, dragging the conversation back to the main issue: 'But what do you think these machines are? Slaves of greater intelligences—robots? Or have the machines indeed beaten men, as Samuel Butler, at the end of the nineteenth century, feared they might?'

'I don't yet pretend to be able to offer any explanation,' Del replied, shaking his head, 'but of one thing I am certain, and that is that they are not robots. You notice, for instance, the irregular finish of this building, both inside and outside. Indisputably, if it had been built by machines, the construction would be mathematically exact. I am convinced that somewhere at the back of all this we shall find a biologically developed intelligence.'

'And it is up to us,' remarked Hale, 'to see that whoever, or whatever, it is doesn't get things all his own way. What weapons have we?'

He and Julian Tyne produced black tubes, which Del and his companions examined with some amusement. Julian appeared nettled.

'What have you?' he asked.

Kal and Ril showed tubes similar to that which Del had lost in the river. They had come prepared with two each.

'Ten times as powerful as yours,' Del explained, 'and for all practical purposes, inexhaustible.'

Roy's revolver was inspected with much the same mirthful contempt as a catapult would have received. Del made an inventory.

'Four high-power heat tubes, two low-power tubes, one solid bullet projector. Not too bad an armoury, though I am sorry that my own heat-ray was lost.'

CHAPTER FOUR

THE 'NUMEN'

THE clang of the metal door roused the whole party from sleep; though how long they had slept, they could not tell. Roy sprang suddenly to a sitting position. He could see by the dim glow that a number of white metal machines were scuttering towards them. Hale was fumbling for his ray tube.

'No,' said Del's voice. 'Your tube has not enough power to hurt them—besides, we are trapped. They may intend no harm.'

The machines advanced with tentacles extended. Roy felt one wrap firmly around his waist and lift him again into the air. It was in his mind to show fight, but Del had advised against it, and he was coming to have a respect for the dwarf's judgment. The rest of the party quietly submitted to like treatment, and were carried towards the still open door.

For a time they passed through corridors in utter blackness. Again they were aware of movement all around them: the clicking and scraping of invisible machines, orderly and un-hurried, as they passed to and fro. At last an arch of daylight showed, wanly and minutely, ahead. Roy breathed a sigh of relief at the prospect of leaving the oppressive gloom of their strange prison. But he was to be disappointed. Forty yards from the passage mouth, the machines stopped, and it was light enough for him to see one of them plunge a feeler into a hole in the wall. There came a familiar clatter as a metal door slid up.

The hall which they now entered was far larger than their former prison, and was lit by the soft, white rays of more than a dozen of the luminous globes. The machines evidently had sufficient knowledge of their prisoners to realise that light was necessary. A surprised exclamation broke from Del. The others, following the line of his pointing finger, observed a row of mechanisms arranged along one wall.

'Our time-travellers!' Hale exclaimed.

Roy identified the remains of his cylinder and Del's dam-aged cage, but was puzzled to see that there were more than a dozen other queer-shaped constructions in company with them.

Without a pause, they were carried on towards a large machine which occupied the centre of the room. Like their bearers, its body-case was ovoid in shape, but unlike them, it possessed no legs and stood half as high again. Save for a pair of lenses and a bunch of metallic tentacles, it lay like a mon-strous egg with a gleaming shell. The prisoners were drawn into a line before it, and the bearers scuttled away, closing the door behind them.

'Well,' said Roy, 'what do you suppose is the next move?'

Del was staring at the machine. Its tentacles were flourishing back and forth, weaving intricate patterns in the air. A hand suddenly grasped Roy's arm. He looked at Jessica Tree, stand-ing beside him.

'What is it——?' he began.

She only pointed. Three shambling figures had emerged from behind the central machine. Roy looked at them amaz-edly, as they came forward to join the party. All three stood well over six feet, superbly muscled and completely naked. Their heads were small, and seemed even smaller above their magnificent chests and the broad spread of their shoulders. A look of bewilderment in their eyes gave way, as they caught sight of Kal and Ril, to relief, mingled with a piteous gladness. They bowed before the two dwarfs in a trustfully submissive manner, and the latter, after momentary confusion, acknowledged the salute by raising their arms in some ancient greeting. Then the three newcomers slouched back a few steps and stood waiting, while Kal and Ril hurriedly conferred.

'Tak Four A?' Kal suggested, cryptically.

'Undoubtedly, but this must have taken many centuries,' answered Ril.

'What are they?' Roy was still regarding the unclassifiable men. Kal offered explanation.

'I imagine they are the result of Tak Four A's artificial selection. He held that we were becoming too atrophied physically —you see we are dwarfs, compared with you—and he decided that a more muscular race, which he proposed to call "Numen," must be created. It looks as if he had been extremely successful.'

'Then these are the masters of the world, now?'

'I don't think so. They seem more confused and surprised than we are.'

He turned and spoke, clearly and carefully, to one of the tall creatures. For a moment the other looked puzzled, then the light of intelligence came into his eyes. He spoke excitedly, and jabbed with a finger in the direction of the derelict time-travellers by the wall.

'So they are in the same jam with us,' mused Roy. 'But surely they could not have built——'

'Certainly they could not,' Kal agreed. 'At a rough guess, I should say they were taught to work the thing and sent on an experimental trip by an inventor who valued his own life.'

Jessica, her first fright abated, looked at them with understanding.

'Poor things,' she murmured. 'For all their size, they're scared to death—frightened, like lost children.'

Del's voice suddenly brought their attention back to the central machine.

'The thing is trying to communicate with us, but we'll never be able to make anything of all that waving of feelers.'

The whole party stared blankly at the writhing tentacles, flashing in meaningless gestures. Abruptly, as though realising that this form of signalling was making no progress, all the feelers save one withdrew and coiled up. The one still extended dropped to the floor and began to scratch a series of queer characters on the earthen surface.

It stopped. The feeler pointed first to them and then to the marks it had made. Del stepped forward and inspected the scratchings more closely. He shook his head. The machine grasped the meaning of the gesture. It smoothed the ground and began again. The characters it produced on the second attempt were undeniably different forms from the first, but were no more intelligible.

Patience was evidently the machine's long suit. Four times it had repeated the smoothing and scratching before they craned over to stare at its moving tentacle in excited silence.

'M,' it wrote.

'M—E—N?'

Del dropped to his knees. Swiftly he traced a large 'YES,' in the dirt.

'HOW?' it asked, after an interval.

Del pointed to the time-travelling machines, and ran across the room to indicate the broken part of his own. The machine understood his meaning, and its feeler fell to scratching what proved to be the beginning of a tedious written conversation.

'For the Lord's sake,' said Roy, some time later, 'tell it to give us some food—we're all in pretty bad need of it!'

The door opened, a few minutes later, in response to some unknown method of communication, and a machine scuttled in bearing circular objects a foot in diameter and three inches thick. Roy picked one up, examined it, and then knocked it experimentally with his knuckles. It gave an unmistakable sound.

'Wood!' he said, disgustedly. 'What the dickens does it think we are? Try it again, Del. Say "fruit" or something like that.'

Some hours later, feeling very much better for the fruit which had been produced in generous quantities, Roy sat beside Jessica and watched the three dwarfs hard at work on one of the time-travellers. The damage to Del's machine had been less serious than he had feared. Such parts as had been ruined could be supplied from the duplicate contrivance in which Kal and Ril had travelled. A couple of hours' toil saw the replacements almost completed.

'Not that it's going to help us any,' said Betty, complainingly. 'You couldn't get more than four into that cage affair, even at a pinch.'

Del agreed. 'But this'—he pointed to the tentacled machine

—'is intelligent. Maybe it can duplicate it for us from a pattern.'

'That's good!' Betty sneered. 'I suppose you're trying to kid me that you're not going to slip off in that traveller and leave us here?'

'We have no intention of doing such a thing.'

Betty shrugged her shoulders and moved away. She favoured Roy with a contemptuous glance as she passed him, and made her way to the side of the moody Hale Lorrence. It was noticeable that, a few minutes later, much of his moodiness had evaporated and the two were deeply engaged in a whispered conversation.

Jessica was puzzled by the relationship between Roy and Betty.

'But I don't understand why you brought her,' she said. 'You're not in love with her.'

Roy agreed, with a slow nod.

'No, I'm not in love with her—not now. But in 1941, I was. She disappeared that year, and for ten years afterwards I devoted myself to building a time-traveller, so that I might find her again. I can see, now, that for all that time I was idealising her. By 1951, I was no longer in love with Betty, but with an ideal girl of my own imagining—a Betty I had built up in my own mind. You understand?'

'I understand. So when you went back to the real Betty...?'

'It was to fetch her from 1941 to 1951. On the return trip, the machine let me down. And,' he added, in a voice so low that she could scarcely hear it, 'I'm glad it did.'

He paused a moment before he went on: 'Tell me, how did you get here—and alone?'

'There's very little to tell. It happened entirely by accident. I had been helping my father to build the machine. Perhaps helping is rather a grand word for the little part I took, but he had no other assistant. My part of the work was far more practical than theoretical. I was very hazy as to the principles of the machine, but I was frequently called upon to make tests of the wiring and connections. Yesterday—thousands of years ago, it is now—I was testing some switches in the traveller. My father must have made the main battery connections and forgotten to warn me. The next thing I knew was that the laboratory had disappeared and there was a sandy plain all around me.

'I realised at once what had happened, and I worked the levers desperately. Nothing responded. I got out of the machine, with an idea of going to find help. Then a red thing came marching over the plain. I was frightened, so I hid as best I could. The thing came up without noticing me. It lifted up the traveller and threw it down on one side, breaking it badly. Then it went on, and I think I lost my head for a time, for I knew I could never mend the machine. I never remember crying in my life before, but I felt so terribly desolate and alone. A little later, the white machines came along and found me.'

'Well, you've got company now, at any rate,' said Roy. 'And I don't think there is any need to be sad. Del will get us back somehow. I've a great faith in that little chap, queer as he looks.'

Hale Lorrence and Betty rose to their feet and began to saunter in the direction of Del and his fellow-workers. After some moments' close examination of the cage, Hale said:

'Your machine is on a slightly different plan from mine. Will you explain it?'

Del indicated the controls and settings, while his assistants put finishing touches to the repairs. Betty climbed into the traveller and began fingering the switches. Roy stopped talking to Jessica and watched. There was a furtiveness about the pair that he did not like. Hale seemed to be edging round, as though he wanted to gain a coveted position. Kal looked up and proclaimed that the work was finished. Immediately, a gleam came into Hale's eyes.

'Look out!' Roy shouted. But he was too late. Like a flash, Hale snatched a high-power heat-ray from Kal's belt.

'Back!' he roared, pointing it at them. 'Back, all of you!'

There was no disobeying the command. Kal and Ril drew ray tubes, but both hesitated to use them—the precious time-traveller stood right behind Hale. As they backed away, the egg-shaped metal creature in the middle of the room stirred its limbs, as though realising what was afoot. One metal tentacle came snaking across the floor towards Hale. Without hesitation, he pressed the catch of his tube and lopped the shining limb away. Another came shooting in his direction, and it too fell to the ground. He turned, and sent a savage jet of heat searing full at the metal body. He swung back, glaring at the group of men; it seemed for a moment that he was minded to end their existences with a final sweep of the heat-beam.

Roy's revolver came into action with a crash. The heavy bullet took Hale in the arm. The tube dropped from his hand, and he bolted into the machine. Roy, as he took aim again, saw the other, unwounded hand reach for the switch. Once more his revolver spurted, but the bullet flattened itself against the wall. The time-traveller, and with it, Hale and Betty, had vanished.

CHAPTER FIVE

THE SECRET OF THE MACHINES

An inarticulate cry, something between a moan and a scream, brought them facing to the centre of the room. One of the Numen was clawing wildly at his body and emitting animal-like howls. Behind him lay the remains of the machine, split by Hale's ray-stroke into two parts. From it a glistening, black tide of life was flowing in their direction. The unfortunate Numan had stood nearest, and already the black flow covered him thickly. Even as they watched in unmoving amazement, he fell writhing to the ground and his body became a mere mound in the blackness.

'Ants!' cried Roy, as the black horde advanced. 'Millions of ants!'

The affrighted group backed up the hall, the two surviving Numen gibbering with fear. Del caught up the tube which Hale had dropped.

'Low power,' he ordered. 'Ray them all.'

There was little need for the command. Kal and Ril were already playing their tubes back and forth across the advancing line, withering the insects by thousands. Julian Tyne, shaken into activity, first by the desertion of his friend and then by the threatening menace, joined in, sweeping his own ray with telling effect.

At every pass they made, thousands of ants shrivelled and became no more than light ash; but still they pushed relentlessly on, marching blindly to certain death. Their centralisation had disappeared with the wreckage of their machine, and now they were left only with the old instinct to attack. There was little real danger; even Julian's lesser ray could have wiped them all out in five minutes. But there came an interruption: the familiar clatter of the metal door. Del turned to see a trio of machines scuttering in through the opening. He pushed up his ray to full power and cut away the fast-moving legs with one sweep. The metal bodies dropped, and impeded those behind.

Del switched a withering blast of heat on the lintel of the

doorway. More by luck than knowledge, he succeeded in melting away the supporting catches, and the metal sheet crashed down, bisecting two entering machines as it fell. Kal sprang to Del's side and trained a ray on one of the stranded machines, turning it incandescent; but already, from the broken halves in the doorway, more black streams of insects were flooding to the attack. Switching his ray to low power lest he should melt the door behind, Del swept a myriad of infuriated ants into eternity. Julian and Ril, behind him, continued the destruction of the first swarm.

Kal dealt rapidly with all three of the powerless machines. Each was rendered red-hot, and its crew incinerated before it could escape. Then he joined Del in repelling the second attack. There came a pandemonium of battering against the door as the machines outside attempted to crash their way in, but the metal sheet was massive enough to defy their most strenuous efforts. The slaughter of the ants was quickly completed. The four tube-holders rayed, on low power, every corner of the great hall, to make certain that none had escaped. Only when they were satisfied that the last ant was wiped out did they have opportunity to pause and consider.

'We'll have to get out of this—and quick!' exclaimed Roy.

'But how? There's no way but the door.'

'Burn our way out,' replied Del. 'We're not far from the open, here. You remember we were near the entrance when they turned in here. Which direction was it?'

'The left wall,' said Roy, definitely. 'But we can't burn through that—all the molten stuff will run back on us in here.'

Del shook his head. 'We can get rid of that.'

A heat-ray was rigged up, pointing directly down at the floor, and then switched on to full power. For ten or twelve seconds the circle of earth below it boiled and seethed furiously, while waves of heat rolled through the cavern. Then, abruptly, it vanished, leaving only a dark hole. Roy stared.

'What happened?' he inquired. Del, switching off the tube, smiled at his astonishment.

'There's no magic about it,' he answered him. 'You see, this place we are in is nothing more or less than a mammoth ant-hill. But ant-hills have workings extending below ground as well as above. We simply melted through the roof of the level below us, and the residue has flowed through the passages down there.'

Approaching as closely as possible, Del began to cut a trench from the foot of the wall to the lip of the newly-drilled hole.

His back was towards the door, and it was only a warning scream from Jessica which saved him from the fate of the luckless Numan. All looked where she pointed. A black carpet of ants was spreading towards them, streaming between the base of the door and the ill-fitting threshold in their hundreds of thousands.

Del turned like a flash, and his tube, still at full power, swept them to instant annihilation. Simultaneously, a corner of the door became a ragged hole in the metal, its edges dripping molten blobs to the floor. Del set Julian to guard the vulnerable spot and turned, with renewed energy, to the drilling of the escape tunnel.

Muffled as much as possible against the heat, he stood back on the far side and trained his ray forward. The solid wall began to liquefy. It oozed and dripped down into the trench he had prepared, flowing along until it poured to unknown depths through the hole in the floor. The operation took no more than a few minutes, but the belching waves of heat reduced them, in even so short a time, to the limit of their endurance. The hot air of the cavern became all but unbreathable. The radiation seemed to scorch them even through their clothing when, to Del's surprise, daylight broke through at ten to a dozen yards distance.

'We've been fortunate,' he remarked, shutting off his tube. 'We were nearer the outside than I suspected. I've drilled the shaft on a slant so that it will drain, but it will be some hours before it is passable. Now we must get to work—when we've made that doorway safe.'

Narrowing his beam, he cut an overhanging piece of the roof so that it fell squarely in front of the hole in the door. Satisfied that the entrance was now completely blocked, he turned his attention to the row of derelict time-travellers.

'These,' he said, with a wave of his hand, 'are the only means we have of regaining our own time. We cannot take them bodily with us. But we must select the more intricate and essential parts, and carry them off. We may be able to discover material for framework, but such things as vacuum tubes, Lestrange batteries, light-impulse cells and the like, would be a great labour to construct—even if we could do so, which is doubtful.'

Very little of Roy's machine was worthy of salvage. When he had extracted his two undamaged Lestrange batteries, he walked over to the two Numen, who were standing helplessly by their crumpled vehicle, and directed them to unbolt such impulse cells as remained intact. Then he became interested in the other machines. Among those unclaimed by anyone present stood two dented metal cubes. Del came over to join him as he pulled on the door of one. It came grudgingly ajar, hanging askew on the twisted frame, and a breath of corruption sent the two men staggering back a pace. Holding his breath, Roy reapproached and peered inside. The shrivelled body of a man, in a far state of decomposition, lay huddled into one of the farther corners.

'Poor devil,' he muttered. 'At least, we've been luckier than he was.'

Del, with his tube at low power, cremated the decaying body, and after waiting a moment for the air to clear, they both entered. One wall was lined with rows of tubes and resistances, while on another were control-panels attended with tortuous convolutions of wiring. Roy peered hopefully among the serried switches and dials for some clue to the machine's date of origin, but without success. Del pondered silently over the mechanism for a while. An expression of wonder came over his face.

'What is it?'

Del answered half to himself. 'I considered it impossible.'

'What do you mean?'

'This vehicle is radically different from ours. It does not plunge instantaneously through the time-flow. Instead, it has the property of slowing down its contents, so that the world ouside slips by at high speed by comparison. A slow, inefficient machine—but it worked.'

'I don't understand.'

'I mean that both our machines, yours and mine, work similarly to the extent that they insulate us entirely from time—that is to say, ages pass by us in a flash and we are not affected. But this is not a complete insulating machine; it works with a kind of drag action. For instance, if the operator turns this main dial to indicate a speed half-way between the normal time-flow and complete insulation, events inside his chamber will take exactly twice as long to happen as they would in the outer world. During the period which seems an hour to him, the events of two hours will take place outside. If he turns the dial farther, the events of a week, or a year, flash past in what appears to be an hour. See, he even has a window through which he can watch the happenings of the world fly past.'

Roy noticed a square of glass set in one wall.

'I think I understand. But what happened?'

'He must have made a mistake somewhere, just as we did; but unlike us, he was travelling so slowly, even at his top speed, that before he reached this date he starved and died on the way—another martyr to experiment. It's a pretty safe guess that we shall find the same fate overtook the man in the other cube.'

Kal came over to summon Del with the information that the salvaged parts had been laid out, awaiting his decision as to which should be taken and which left. Under his direction, the selected fragments were divided among the party for portage. A further inspection of the passage revealed that it was still too hot for use; they must wait at least another hour. Del looked worried, and examined the joints of floors and walls carefully for any traces of the ants breaking through.

'Ants,' said Roy, musingly, as they waited. 'Insects working those machines—ruling the world, perhaps. It's incredible.'

'It's logical,' Del contradicted.

'I don't get that.'

'It was inevitable, sooner or later. They've always had a far better organisation than man, even in my century—no wasted effort, no need to struggle continually with subversive factors. The only thing which stopped them being masters of the world, from the beginning, was their size. Now, they have found a way of overcoming that disability. There's a natural limit to the size of insects. They do not breathe as we do, but absorb the oxygen through the surface. If they became large, there would not be enough absorption area in proportion to the bulk inside, and they would die of suffocation.'

'Yes, I see that. But to find them working machines—and such machines—just staggers me.'

'But why? It's the natural way out of the difficulty. After all, we did the same. Where would man have been without his machines? If you want a parallel, just think of one of the warships of your own time—twelve hundred or more men working a great floating monster, just as these insects in their thousands work their scuttering metal machines. It puzzles me that I didn't think of it the moment we saw the style of their machines. But these things always seem so obvious afterwards.'

Roy nodded. 'But, still, I would never have believed if I hadn't seen,' he added.

A rattle of falling dirt startled the group. They looked apprehensively upward. A shining metal tentacle protruded through a small hole in the room. An increasing rain of debris pattered all about them as it moved from side to side, enlarging the aperture.

Kal's tube sent a shaft of heat shooting up. Either from haste or misjudgment, he had it notched at full-power. The tentacle was melted off, and fell, but the heat-beam had seared on into the roof. There came an ominous cracking, and the men, with a startled glance, took to their heels in the direction of the escape tunnel. Almost as they drew clear, the weakened spot gave way and the machine, with an avalanche of dirt, crashed to the floor. Even as it broke open, rivers of ants came swarming out of the gaping seams. With a second crash, another machine fell through the hole, and after it, another. It seemed that the insects cared little how many machines were wrecked to secure the victory.

'Into the tunnel!' shouted Del. 'We must risk it, now.'

The rest scampered to obey, holding their precious burdens in their arms. Kal charged ahead with his weapon held ready and his short legs moving with twinkling rapidity. The others followed him closely. Roy heard a howl of agony break from the two Numen as their bare feet encountered the hot surface, but their fear of the ants was greater than their discomfort, and they held on their way.

The heat of the passage was intense; it beat at them like a furnace glare. Jessica staggered just ahead of Roy. He caught her around the waist with his free arm, and dragged her on. The two of them pitched together over the outer edge into the daylight—he had forgotten that the slant of the tunnel meant a six-foot drop at the other end. Del had remained till the last. He rayed furiously at the increasing horde of ants until he was sure that his companions were clear; then he, too, turned and ran for safety. He fell from the tunnel's mouth, narrowly missing the prostrate Roy.

'Only a dozen yards of that inferno,' said the latter, sitting up, 'yet it seemed like a hundred. Anyhow, it's a sight too hot for the ants to get across it. We're clear of them for a bit.'

Del agreed, but he wished to make sure. 'Lift me up on your shoulders,' he directed. Roy did so, and the dwarf played a narrow ray on the sloping passage roof till it fell, completely closing the entrance.

'Any casualties?' Roy inquired, as he lowered the other.

'No, except these two.' Jessica pointed to the two Numen, who were sitting down ruefully examining their scorched soles. 'And they're more surprised than hurt. But I should think,' she added, 'that the vacuum tubes have suffered.'

A hurried inspection revealed that only one had been smashed.

'And now, where do we go from here?' Roy asked Del, who, by general consent, had become director of the party.

'We get away very quickly, before they realise what has happened and start a search for us,' Del replied.

It took but a short time to cross the open ground and gain the cover of the forest. Roy, looking back for a final view of the rearing cliffs which formed the side of the stupendous ant-hill, was relieved to discern no signs of pursuit.

CHAPTER SIX

THE DAY OF THE INSECT

SEVERAL hours of heavy going found them a weary party. The three dwarfs had very soon given out; their small bodies were of little use for this kind of rough going. One of the Numen, noticing their distress, handed his bundle over to his fellow and, as though it were the most natural thing in the world, raised Kal and Ril to his broad shoulders. The other placed both bundles upon one shoulder and seated Del on the other.

'That proves it!' declared Kal, as he recovered from his surprise. 'These are the descendants of Tak Four A's Numen. Brawn, developed to assist brains.'

For some miles they had proceeded along the bed of a stream, with the dual purpose of losing the scent and of making slightly easier progress than was possible among the trees. On a corner, the leading Numan stopped short. Roy craned round him to ascertain the cause, and found himself staring at one of the six-legged machines. It stood motionless on the grass verge of the left bank, glistening in the sunlight.

Del pulled out his tube, but as he levelled it, the machine became aware of them and scurried swiftly sideways. For a moment it paused, waving its tentacles slightly, as though uncertain whether to attack or not; then it flashed away into the trees and out of sight.

'Damn it!' said Roy, as he watched the last glitter of the receding shell. 'It will give the alarm.' Rather bitterly, he added: 'Why didn't you melt the thing?'

'Because I had no desire to set the whole forest on fire,' Del replied calmly.

Tired as they were, they pressed on with greater speed. They must, Del pointed out, reach some defensible spot. While they remained among the trees, they were liable to concealed attack from any side. Another two hours brought them to a district where open spaces were more frequent, but still Del was unsatisfied. At the edge of a sizeable clearing, Roy demurred.

'Jessica's dead beat, Julian's very little better, and I've had enough, too. We'll find nothing to beat this. If we camp in the middle, we can defend all round'

Julian upheld the suggestion in a tired, dispirited voice. Del opened his mouth, but before he could speak there came an interruption.

'Get into the trees, you fools!' roared a voice. For a second, nobody moved. 'I mean it,' called the voice, somewhere above their heads. 'They're coming after you. Get moving!'

The tone was so insistent that, this time, they obeyed without question. As Roy, who was the last to climb, swung himself up the branches, he heard the approach of a multitudinous scuttering. Looking down, he could see the flashing surfaces of a dozen or more passing ant-machines.

'Close call,' said a voice above him.

'Certainly was—and it'd have been a damn sight closer if you hadn't been about,' Roy answered softly.

'It's all right; you needn't whisper. Those tin things can't hear. I've tried 'em. What's more, they're too dumb to look for anything up above 'em. You're safe here.'

Roy leaned back and looked up at the speaker on his higher branch. He was a man of knotty, compact build, clad in a torn shirt and ill-used khaki trousers. The greater part of his face was hidden beneath an unruly growth of black beard and whiskers, but his mouth smiled, and there was a zestful twinkle in his eyes. Roy climbed higher and stretched out his hand. It was taken in a hardened, calloused grip.

'You can't guess how glad I am to see you folks, whoever you are. I reckoned I'd got the world to myself, 'cept for them crawlin' tin cans down there. I'm Jim Hollis. About four days ago, I was somewhere near Indianapolis—the Lord knows where I am now!'

Roy introduced himself. He added: 'Do you know of any safe place for us? We're mostly about played out.'

Jim Hollis scratched his chin reflectively through his matted beard. He cast a glance towards the Sun, now well in the west.

'Can you make two miles—maybe, two and a half?' he inquired.

'If it's worth while, I guess we could manage that.'

'It's worth while, all right. There's some caves I found in a cliff over there.' He jerked his head in an easterly direction. 'I'd be there now, myself, but I couldn't make the entrance on my own. Way up above my head.'

'It can be defended?' asked Del, from a branch near-by.

The man looked curiously at the dwarf. 'Sure,' he agreed, 'but it don't need it. If I couldn't make the grade, I'm damned if one of them tin things could. If we're goin', we'd better move right now. It'll be sunset in a couple of hours.'

He swung himself down the branches and dropped to the ground. The rest of them followed his lead. The dwarfs' true proportions were revealed when they had descended, and at sight of them and the accompanying Numen, the man's eyes widened with amazement.

'Say, what the——?' he began.

Roy tactfully interposed. 'Lead on,' he said. 'I'll tell you as we go.'

'You'll have to. I'm all dazed up. It's all happened so sudden-like. I was just hiking along, hoping to jump a truck-ride to Indianapolis, when a guy comes out from a shack by the road-side and says he'll give me five bucks if I'll lend him a hand. I'd clean forgot what five bucks looks like, so I said I would. He'd got a piece of machinery he couldn't move by himself, and he wanted it brought out of the shack into the yard. Rummy lookin' sort of cage, with a sling-seat in it. We got it out easy enough between us, and then he went back to find the five bucks, so I sat down in the sling-seat. There was a lot of little switches and thingummies in front of it, so I pressed one, just interested like. Next thing I knew, me and the machine was crashin' down through a lot of branches like these.'

He looked disparagingly at the growths about him. 'And they ain't even ordinary trees. Nothin's ordinary around these parts—what's more, I ain't got my five bucks.'

Roy attempted to explain the situation, and to tell how the rest of them had similarly come to grief. Jim Hollis grunted doubtfully.

'Sounds crazy to me,' he observed, 'but then, it's no crazier than having them tin things runnin' about the place. Ants inside of 'em, you say?'

'Yes, ants.'

Jim sniffed. He was still a trifle uncertain whether this might not be some deep scheme to pull his leg.

'And what about the big red things that walk on two legs? What's in them—black beetles?'

Roy had forgotten the red machines. He smiled at Jim's suggestion, and admitted that none of the party had yet had an opportunity of investigating these inhabitants of this strangely transformed world.

Jim's estimate of two miles was modest by half, but they came at length, and without hesitation, to the edge of the forest. Across a hundred yards of turf rose a cliff-face, pitted in many places with dark holes.

'How's that?' asked Jim, triumphantly pointing to the largest. It measured some ten feet in diameter at the entrance.

'But how do we get there?' Julian objected, looking at the twenty-five feet of sheer cliff which must be scaled.

'Easy enough to reach it by standing on one another's shoulders.'

'I have a better idea than that,' said Del. He produced a ray tube and, with a series of heat-jets, drilled a zig-zag line of holes up the rock face.

'Gee! That's a dandy flashlight you've got,' Jim murmured admiringly.

Roy ascended the holds, after a short interval for cooling. As a precaution, he took with him a heat-ray set ready at low-power. The first glance showed him that the cave was both empty and dry. It broadened out to about fifteen feet, a yard or two inside the entrance, and ran back nearly thirty feet into the cliff. Luck had favoured them with an ideally safe refuge. He stood up at the mouth and looked out towards the setting Sun.

'It's okay,' he called to the group of upturned faces. 'Come on, all of you! Back to the Stone Age!'

'The problems of food and water have been easily settled,' said Del, addressing the group on the following day. 'It is indeed lucky for us that fruit grows in such profusion, but though this will keep us alive, it will not assist us to solve the problem of our return. For that, one thing is essential—we must have metal.'

Roy looked up from his occupation of plaiting creeper strands into a rope.

'I was wondering what you intended to do about that,' he remarked.

'What's the metal for?' asked Jim.

'We must have a framework for the machine which I propose to build—and it must be a metal framework. You want to get back, don't you?'

'Sure I do. That guy still owes me five bucks.'

'What kind of metal?' Roy inquired.

Del shrugged his shoulders. 'A steel containing chromium and tungsten in small quantities would be best; failing that, some other hard metal could be made to serve. I also want some copper, or other good conductors. Very luckily, most of our salvaged parts have withstood the journey.' Turning to Jim, he added: 'Is your machine still in the branches where it fell?'

'No; the tin things found it and carried it off. I watched them from a tree.'

Reflectively, Del looked out of the cave towards the giant ant-hill towering over the trees in the distance. Jim's arrival accounted for one of the extra time-travellers they had seen there. He wondered about the others ... Jim's voice broke in on the unprofitable speculation.

'Maybe, if we scouted round a bit more, we might find a town or something. Anyway, there ought to be a road leading to a town—and where there's a town, there's sure to be metal.'

Del shook his head gently. 'You don't realise. There are no towns.'

'No towns?'

'Neither towns, nor men.'

'You're foolin' me! They can't all be dead.'

'They must be, or the insects would not be ruling.'

'But—do you mean the ants have killed all the men?'

'It seems unlikely. Probably men just stopped.'

'I don't get you.'

'Men did not kill off the great reptiles who ruled the world before them—the reptiles just stopped. It seems to me that man, too, has "had his little day and ceased to be." '

'But what's the good of his ever havin' lived, if it all finishes this way?'

'What is the use of life? Perhaps man came to a glorious finish, fulfilled his destiny and vanished from the Earth—he had to leave the Earth sooner or later. At least, he has not been compelled to linger on a globe which is drifting into senile decay.'

'It doesn't look decaying to me.' Jim gazed out at the gently swaying trees.

'But we found ourselves in a desert when we stopped. Miles of it, overlaying what once was fruitful country.... How far did that desert stretch? For all we know, this may be an oasis of forest in a world of deserts. And have you noticed the Sun—how much larger and more fiery red it is than our accustomed Sun? Signs of the coming end, both of them.'

He was silent for a moment before he added: 'Then there was the ant-machine which questioned us. Its knowledge of the past must have been profound, yet it tried us with a series of symbols utterly unknown to any of us. One wonders what strange creatures used those symbols, some time between the end of man and the rise of the insect. Yes; we are far past the age of *homo sapiens. . . .'*

No one spoke for a while. It was Roy who broke the spell.

'This is morbid,' he declared. 'Our present concern is to regain the age of *homo sapiens*—and our immediate need is metal.'

Jessica, sitting beside him, drew a breath as though to speak, and then changed her mind.

'Yes?' he encouraged.

'I hardly like to suggest it. I mean, it's dangerous.'

'What is it?'

'Well, the ants' white machines——'

'Yes?'

'Well, they must be made of a very hard metal.'

Roy brought his hand down on his knee with a slap of approval.

'Good girl, you've hit it! We've got to grab one of those machines, somehow or other.'

The expeditionary force eventually comprised only three men: Roy, Jim Hollis and Julian. The two Numen would have been useful but, since it was considered unwise to trust them with heat-rays, they would have been defenceless in case of an attack. They would, therefore, be summoned later to help with the portage, if necessary. Moreover, it was important that some weapons should be left with the rest of the party, in case of trouble. Both Roy and Jim, before they left, were handed high-power rays and instructed in the use of them. Julian retained his own, low-power weapon.

'What puzzles me is how we are going to attract the things,' Roy said.

'Forget it. There's no attractin' needed,' Jim assured him. 'All we've got to do is get up a tree near a clearing, and wait. They'll come along soon enough. It's dollars to dough-nuts we spot some within a couple of hours. Them tin things are for ever snoopin' around—the Lord knows what for.'

They progressed cautiously, with Jim in the lead, scanning the surrounding growths for the slightest sign of a metallic flash, and ready to jump for the branches. The chosen clearing, a mile or so distant, was reached without alarms. There, they climbed one of the loftiest trees and settled themselves among the boughs to wait. After an hour of patience, Roy caught the sound of activity on the far side of the open space. As it approached, it resolved itself into a crackling of branches

accompanied by a faint clanking. He moved into an attitude
of readiness, and slipped the ray tube out of his pocket. Jim
put out a restraining hand.

'It ain't the tin things. It's the big, red brutes. I know the
sound of 'em.'

The next minute proved him right. Five of the twenty-foot
machines left the trees and stalked stiffly on their trellised legs
across the other end of the clearing.

'Five again,' Roy murmured.

'Always five together—never more, nor less. And if I know
anything about it, it means that some of the ant-machines are
around these parts.' Jim replied.

Less than ten minutes after the red stalkers had disappeared,
there came a flash of reflected sunlight among the trees. A
moment later, no less than ten of the six-legged machines
emerged. They paused in a bunch, and there was a great waving of silver tentacles. Roy wondered why it was that the
machines were not rendered less conspicuous with a coating of
neutral-shaded paint; it was merely one of many puzzling
points about them.

As a result of the conference, the party broke up. Eight
scurried away in the wake of the red monsters; another
doubled back the way they had come, while the remaining one
retreated to the shadow of the trees and stood motionless. Jim
nudged Roy.

'There's our meat,' he said.

CHAPTER SEVEN

CASTAWAYS IN A DEAD WORLD

WITH stealth and care, they wriggled back along the branches
and slid to the ground. Keeping about twenty yards back from
the edge of the clearing, they began to work round into pos-
tion. The fact that their progress was accompanied by a considerable crackling of twigs underfoot did not worry them, but
it was essential that no waving of bushes, carelessly brushed
aside, should attract the attention of the sharp lenses. Moreover, a look-out must be kept for other roving machines. At
fifty yards' range, Jim suggested that they take to the trees
again.

Roy, through a leafy gap, trained his ray on the motionless
sentry, and pressed the catch. His aim was good. A quick

switch of the wrist from left to right, and the narrow blade of intense heat scythed the legs from beneath it. It fell with a thud. The tentacles writhed for a few seconds, and then dropped, to lie listlessly on the ground. As they sank, the ant army came surging from its fallen craft. Roy swiftly adjusted his tube to lower power and wider aperture, and joined Jim and Julian, who were already fanning their beams at the black flood. In a few moments, the insects had withered from sight, and the damaged machine was theirs.

Roy swung down from the tree, and advanced with his tube cautiously levelled against the possibility of another rush of ants. He tapped experimentally on the metal casing, but none emerged. Again he set his ray to a small aperture, preparatory to slicing the metal into portable sections. Barely had he raised the tube when there came a cry from Jim, who pointed wildly across the clearing.

Roy spun round, to see two more white machines headed in a scuttering dash towards him. He swung his ray without hesitation, and brought down the leader. Its own momentum sent it sliding a dozen yards on its shining belly. As it fell, he turned his attention to the other. But the second attacker was not destined to fall such an easy victim.

He was raising his hand when a metal tentacle from behind him snapped around his body, knocking his weapon spinning towards the tree. He realised, as the arm gripped him, that he had been fooled. Some of the ants still remained in the first machine, and had successfully played 'possum until this moment. He cursed himself for not having the foresight to put its lenses out of action.

The trees behind him literally exploded into flame, as the tube fell among them. Jim and Julian leaped from their perches with lightning agility, and came pounding to Roy's defence with ready weapons. The last, unharmed machine, dashing on with tentacles extended, was almost upon him. Their line of fire was masked by Roy's body. He tugged frenziedly at his metal bond, but it had frozen into inflexibility, holding him as prey for the other.

Jim decided to take a desperate chance. He steadied, and aimed. The searing heat-beam passed within inches of the helpless Roy, and the hot air scorched his face, but the blast passed on to shear the legs from one side of the rushing monster. The unsupported side fell with a crash, and the machine swivelled wildly to one side. It rolled over and over, till it came to a final rest within a yard of Roy's feet. But the danger was far from over. Jim bounded towards him, fused the restraining tentacle at its base, and dragged him free just as the swarming ants broke from their wrecked craft. Only then did the three men become aware of the great flames licking out from the blazing trees towards them.

'We've got to get out of this quick. We've sure started something this trip,' said Jim, as Roy unwrapped the severed tentacle. 'The Lord knows what that tube will do, now it's on the loose. All the walkin' tin cans in this crazy world are likely to happen along, just to see who's been jokin' around here.'

'But the metal——'

'Damn the metal. There's plenty more—we can't move fast and carry the stuff. Till this blows over, we can go home and lie doggo for a bit.'

The three crossed the clearing at top speed. In the shelter of the opposite trees, they paused to look back. A vast funnel of flame was belching into the heavens and, above it, thick clouds of smoke broadened, mushroom-like. Jim shook a rueful head.

'Ain't that just our darned luck?' he growled.

There followed several weeks, uneventful to the castaways. Roy and Jim had returned to the scene of their fight, on the following day, and made encouraging discoveries. The first was that the fire started by Roy's lost tube had spread only a very little distance beyond its raging centre. With no wind to fan them, the flames had dwindled away, and finally snuffed out. The tube itself was irretrievably lost, somewhere in a crater of its own making. It had melted the ground and the rocks beneath it, and sunk out of sight into the molten pool. Whether it had destroyed itself, or whether it was still digging deeper and deeper into the earth, neither of the men knew, nor cared to any extent. They were far too elated at finding that the machines they had vanquished still lay where they had fallen.

'Wonder why they haven't taken them away?' Roy had said. Jim snorted.

'You're always wondering about the things. What's the use of tryin' to get inside an insect's mind, anyway? You couldn't do it in a life-time. Maybe they never repair—only build new machines. The thing that counts, now, is that here's the metal just waiting for us to carry it off.'

With the help of most of the party, the transport had been successfully accomplished; though more than once on the journey it was necessary to drop their burdens and take to the trees, to avoid wandering machines. A growing acquaintance with the dangers of the world about them, and with the limited capabilities of their enemies, began to have a tonic effect on the party. Jim Hollis had never shown anything more than contempt for what he called 'walking tinware,' and the rest were fast adopting his point of view.

Del, with Kal for an assistant, had gone to work right away on the construction of a new time-traveller, once he had assured himself that the metals were suitable. Ril, whose offers of assistance had been refused on the ground that more than one helper would lead to confusion, busied himself in experimenting with the least damaged of the captured machines, a pursuit in which he was joined by Julian. Jim Hollis was appointed head of the foraging staff and, with the help of the two Numen, saw that a plentiful supply of fruit and water was maintained.

Jessica and Roy found themselves much together. Since the ant-machines were seldom to be seen in the immediate vicinity of the cliffs, they had formed the habit of taking their strolls in the neighbourhood. Roy, after a month or more of this existence, had come to accept their way of life as a commonplace rather than an adventure. He discovered, with a sense of surprise, that Jessica did not share this view.

'How long,' she asked him one morning, 'do you think it will be before Del completes his machine?'

Roy looked at her doubtfully. There was something in her tone that he could not place. It was not exactly an eagerness for release from this strange world, and yet . . .

'Not more than a day or two, now, I believe; but he is not sure that some further adjustments won't be necessary. You're feeling homesick?'

Jessica failed to reply for a moment. She held her gaze fixed straight ahead, and there was a slight petulance in the line of her mouth. At length she answered, in a dull voice:

'I suppose I am. After all, one could hardly wish to stay here for ever. Sometimes, at nights, it comes over me in a perfect wave of longing. I look out and see nothing but the dimness of the stars, and hear nothing but the stirring of the trees; then I long for our bustling twenty-third century. I want to see the sky split by the green fire at the tail of an Asia-bound rocket, or the red gush from the Europe express.

'Sometimes, on clear nights, we could see from our house the pure-white flames streaming from the Mars space-ship as it spurted from its cradle. And then, too, there was never this terrible quiet. Even when one was shut away, there was always a sense of movement, of a world where men and their machines all worked to some purpose—a rustling sense of life

even in the quietest places. I feel a horrible sense of futility
that it has all come only to this—to the insects.'

'I'm sure you are wrong there. If we had found men still
existing at this date, I should feel that it did seem futile. It
would mean that man must die when the world dies. But,
since there is no sign of him, I am convinced that he achieved
his true end—whatever that may have been—and gone on his
way, leaving the world to other forms of life so that they may
in turn achieve their ends.'

'I think you are an optimist, Roy, but I hope you are right. I
confess, I don't feel very cheerful about anything just now.'

'While I seem to feel happier than I ever remember, I could
almost hope that Del's machine should turn out a failure. I
wish . . .' He stopped abruptly. A light crept into Jessica's eyes.
The corners of her mouth lifted, ever so slightly.

'Yes?' she prompted, gently. But Roy was not looking; he
did not see the change that had come over her.

'I don't know. It seems so unnecessary that we should go
back to our own centuries—and yet, we must.'

'Must?'

'Well, imagine what a misfit I should be in Del's century.'

Jessica sighed to herself over the obtuseness of men. 'I can't
imagine you in Del's century,' she said. But Roy missed the
emphasis which was laid upon the word 'Del,' and took the
statement at its face value. Jessica let the subject drop. She had
learned what she wanted to know; the rest was a matter of
careful handling. She might even have to propose herself, in
the end. . . .

Half an hour later, as they were returning to the cave, Roy
announced that there was a surprise awaiting her. Ril and
Julian, in their experiments with the captured ant-machine,
had succeeded in making it workable. The machinery cased in
the lower part of the ovoid body, and partitioned off, had been
found to be intact. It had not been a great labour, with the
help of the heat-rays, to braise on salvaged legs in place of
those shorn away. Then, more to give themselves employment
than for any other reason, the two men had set about adapting
the controls for human use. To this end, they had applied
themselves to the solution of a number of ingenious problems
which turned out, in most cases, less difficult than they had
expected. Much of the work consisted merely of clearing away
many of the stages necessary for insect manipulation.

'What I mean is,' said Roy, explaining, 'a man might need a
block and tackle to lift a heavy log which an elephant would

lift direct. This time, Ril and Julian were in the position of the elephant—they could dispense with much of the intermediate mechanical aid. They're as pleased with the thing as a child with a new toy. It's going to be ready to show off its tricks when we get back.'

'But what's the good of it?'

'None, I think. They merely felt an interest in the thing, and it gave them something to do. They solved it as one might solve any other puzzle. You'll see it soon.'

His words were borne out, a few hundred yards from home. They saw the glittering machine approach, slowly scrabbling over the ground towards them. It stopped as they came into view, and stood still, its tentacles waving in the usual manner of the ant-operated craft. Roy gave a chuckling laugh.

'A pretty good imitation. If I hadn't been expecting it, I'd have rayed the thing right off—and that would have been very uncomfortable for Ril and Julian.'

As if at the thought, his hand went to his belt. It encountered the butt of his revolver, but the ray tube was missing. He cursed his carelessness in not bringing it; such an omission might well have had tragic results. He and Jessica advanced together.

'Now, Ril, put it through its paces,' he called. But the machine merely stood there, waving its tentacles. A sudden misgiving shot through Roy's mind. To reassure himself, he called: 'What are you trying to do? Scare us?'

Jessica drew closer to his side. She was aware of an uncomfortable sense that all was not well.

'Suppose it isn't——?' she began. She got no further, for at that moment the machine snapped into action. It came scuttering full at them, tentacles outstretched.

'Run!' cried Roy, but instead, she shrank towards him. He jerked out his revolver and spat a burst of ineffective shots. The machine charged down on them. A feeler wrapped about Jessica's waist and snatched her from his side; another looped about his wrist, dragging him along. With a violent twist of his arm, he broke its grip and fell to the ground. Jessica screamed as the metal legs thudded past within inches of his head. The machine did not wait to recapture him; holding the girl clear of the ground, it made straight for the trees. Roy grabbed for his fallen revolver, jumped to his feet and raced vainly after it. The danger of hitting Jessica was too great for him to risk a shot, and the machine, looking like some great, shining beetle, was travelling twice his speed. The girl gave one final, despairing cry; then captor and captive disappeared among the branches.

For a few dazed seconds, Roy continued to run, before his senses reasserted themselves and sent him shouting in the direction of the cave. Consternation reigned in the group as he panted out his news.

'Give me a ray tube,' he demanded. 'I'll wreck that machine and bring Jessica back, if it's the last thing I do.'

Del caught his arm. 'You could never catch it before it reached the ant-hill, and it's no good trying single-handed to——'

Ril broke in. He had exchanged a hurried whisper with Julian, which sent the other running towards the cave.

'We'll take the machine,' he said. 'Julian and I have finished it and tested it.'

Roy, without hesitation, dashed to the spot where the renovated craft lay, and started hurling aside the branches which masked it. Ril clambered up a rough ladder set against the side, and slid into the interior through a hole in the top.

'Tubes—we must have them,' Roy called. Del handed over two high-power tubes and one low one. The only remaining tube he retained, in case of attack.

'Get the girl back, and we will go,' he said. 'The timetraveller will be ready when you return.'

Julian came running back with an armful of additional apparatus. which he lugged aboard. Roy slid in last, and slapped the covering panel shut. Ril and Julian were already at the controls. The machine stirred with a slight lurch; then, with metal legs flashing in the sunlight, it scuttered at full speed for the trees and the spire of the giant ant-hill beyond them.

CHAPTER EIGHT

THE CENTRAL INTELLIGENCE

For the first hour, silence was scarcely broken. Ril could spare no attention from the delicate occupation of steering the unfamiliar machine, and Julian was engaged in arranging some of the apparatus he had so hurriedly gathered. Noticeable among it was the lamp which they had used to light the cave. Roy moved restlessly about the confined space, peering through one or another of the observation holes which had been pierced in the metal hull. Continually he turned to urge Ril to greater speed. The dwarf shook his head. Already they were at the speed limit of safe travel, and time and again he avoided a crash with some tree only by the swiftest dexterity.

The greatest concern which beset him was lest they should reach some unfordable stream and be forced to a long detour, but the fear was unfounded. The first water they encountered was a clear brook, flowing rapidly over a shallow bed of stones, and without hesitation, they took it in a shower of sparkling drops. As they were mounting the further bank, the first untoward incident occurred; there came a mighty crash to one side, and a tree toppled slowly. It missed them as it fell by only a few feet. Another crash, close at hand, caused Ril to steer the machine hastily to the right. Roy was flung to the floor by the sudden change of direction.

'What was that?' he demanded, as he scrambled up.

'Rocks,' said Ril briefly. 'They nearly got us, too.'

Roy remembered the scene they had witnessed on the day of their arrival.

'It's the red things. They've spotted us! Here, give me a ray.'

He thrust his head and shoulders out of the top panel, and looked about him. No enemy was visible, but away ahead he could hear the crackling of branches as something drew nearer.

'Coming this way. Move off a bit.'

Ril obeyed speedily and, a moment later, a rock landed on the spot where they had paused. Roy guessed that they must have been seen as they made the crossing, and that the rocks were being thrown by guess-work. A red machine stalked into view and halted uncertainly. The silver ant-craft was now effectively screened from its view by a clump of bushes. A second presently joined it. Roy hesitated only for a second— with Jessica still at stake, they could afford to waste no time; he lifted the ray tube. One sweep sliced off a trellised leg, and the machine, as it tottered, fell against its companion. The two swayed for a space, and then went down together with a resounding crash and a furious flailing of their jointed arms.

'Right away—flat out,' Roy called, and Ril threw in the lever which sent them scurrying on their course.

The red machines were about the countryside in unusual numbers, they discovered as they continued; but further direct encounters were successfully avoided. Moreover, as they drew nearer to the ant-hill, they began to meet with an increasing number of machines similar to their own. These, at first, they gave a wide berth, but it soon became obvious that they had no need to fear molestation, since the ants gave no sign of suspecting their presence.

They were still some two miles from the hill when Roy, at a forward peep-hole, gave an excited cry. Disappearing into the trees on the far side of a clearing, he had caught a glimpse of Jessica's captor, with her form still closely wrapped in its tentacles. Ril urged them at full speed across the open ground and plunged into the forest, hard on the track. But despite his utmost efforts, it was not until they emerged into the space ringing the base of the ant-hill that they caught another glimpse of the marauder.

Their gain had been appreciable, and Roy decided to risk a ray flash; they could not hope to overtake the other before it reached the dark entrance to the hill. His ray, at low power, flashed on the twinkling legs with no result. He pushed the power up a notch, and tried again. This time he succeeded in fusing one of the rear leg-joints, so that the metal limb became rigid. Unfortunately, it projected clear, and hampered progress not at all. The tube was just levelled for a third shot when a hand grasped his wrist, and he turned to face Julian. The latter spoke angrily.

'Put that away, you fool!' he snapped. 'Can't you see that if you did bring the thing down, it would most likely kill Jessica in the fall? Even if it didn't, she'd be covered with ants in a few seconds.'

The possibility shook Roy badly; he cursed his own foolhardiness as he returned the tube to his belt. Julian turned his back and began to adjust the lamp, now erected at one of the larger spy-holes. A minute later, the leading machine, still clutching Jessica, disappeared into the dark mouth of the entrance. After it, all six legs threshing furiously, pounded the avenger.

Julian pressed a switch, and a beam of dazzling brilliance bored down the tunnel before them. The vast central roadway stretched out like a dirigible hangar of infinite length. Here and there, the upsweeping curves of the walls were pierced with side-turnings; mysterious, gaping mouths whose immenseness was dwarfed only by the proportions of the main artery. Of traffic, there was little at the present, but such machines as were visible scuttled along with a methodical orderliness, keeping to the right of the track and paying no attention either to pursuer or pursued.

'Why don't they attack us?' Roy wondered.

'Too specialised,' replied Ril. 'Their whole organisation is worked on a basis of calculation, precision and instinct. They know, for instance, that there is danger from the red stalking-machines outside; that danger is calculated and allowed for. But when they face us, they are up against the incalculable, and their instincts are not any help to them. For centuries, perhaps, they have not been called upon to cope with the unexpected.'

'But they attacked and captured us in the first place.'

'True, but then they were in the open, where dangers might be expected and their instinct was to overcome a challenge. It requires more than instinct and simple calculation to grasp the idea of one of their own machines being turned against them. You notice that even the one we are following has shown no sign of perturbation; it has just kept steadily on its way and paid no attention to anything else.'

'Then we are safe from interference? All we have to do is to recapture Jessica when we reach the other machine, and march out with her.'

Ril looked doubtful. It seemed unlikely that it would be as simple as that.

'We are all right, I think, until we are discovered by the central intelligence. We can't tell what will happen then.'

'But how do you know there is a central intelligence?'

Ril lifted one hand from the controls of the racing vehicle, and waved it in an expressive sweep.

'Something must control all this. Besides, you remember the machine which wrote on the floor—it was obviously designed for brain-work of some kind. It had no legs to move about on. It was a calculating machine—a kind of composite-thinking mechanism. Somewhere in this ant-mountain there must be a super-calculator, capable not only of working from known factors, but of reasoning from probabilities; a kind of central brain, of which our questioner was a mere subsidiary.'

'It sounds too improbable.'

'I don't think so. Since the insects had even more natural obstacles to overcome than man had, they must, of necessity, use more involved apparatus.'

While Ril spoke, they gradually gained on the machine ahead. Now, a bare twenty yards separated the two. Julian already had his hands on the control-levers of the tentacles, and was ready to send them coiling out the moment the range permitted. The leader turned, with a sudden swerve, down a passage to the left. Only by skilful manipulation did Ril avoid overshooting the corner, but he succeeded, and they gained yet another couple of yards. The three men grew more tense as the distance lessened. Julian's knuckles were white on the levers, and his face strained. Roy again thrust his head and shoulders through the top panel, and held his tube ready for action. Then, with disconcerting suddenness, the passage walls fell away and they sped out into a large, circular hall.

Roy had a glimpse of serried ranks of the white metal machines, gleaming and glittering in the rays of their lamp; then his eyes rose to the structure which dominated the whole vast room. It stood, raised on a dais in the exact centre—a huge, metallic shape, sprouting with a multitude of shining feelers. At that moment, Julian went into action. Judging his distance to a nicety, he sent a tentacle whipping round one of the rear legs of Jessica's captor.

Simultaneously, Ril slowed their machine, and there came a jerk which almost dislodged Roy from his perch. The legs of the leader crumpled beneath it, and the shining belly met the ground with a thud. Julian, with the full power of the attached tentacle, began to draw it back towards them. From his vantage-point, Roy sliced with a pencil-thick ray at the roots of the feelers which bound Jessica. The whole affair had taken place so quickly that they had been unmolested; but as the last strand parted, there came an ominous stirring in the ranks of the surrounding machines.

Ril's voice rose insistently. 'Quick! Get that central globe!'

Roy perceived that the many feelers around it had sprung into furiously writhing signals. With sweeps of his ray at full power, he carved it into sections. As the parts fell, he saw the outflow of myriads of ants, running in glistening streams across the floor.

'Too late!' cried Ril. 'It's given the order.'

Roy swung his beam around the closing circle of machines, while the tentacles under Julian's control sought and grasped the prostrate form of Jessica. They snatched her from the ground a split second before the insect hordes swept the spot.

'We've got to run for it,' Ril called up, as he manoeuvred their craft to the right-about. 'Clear a way to the passage.'

The few machines in their path were swiftly dealt with, but while Roy's attention was taken aside, the rest of the circle was closing in.

'Full speed!' he roared down to the dwarf.

They tore forward with a jerk, the light and Roy's heat-ray blazing ahead of them. Once in the comparative safety of the corridor, he turned around and devoted his attention to hindering the pursuit. Dozens fell to his ray, but he saw that, in spite of his destruction, the mass was gaining. At a sudden idea, he thrust the power of his tube down a couple of notches, and gave an exclamation of satisfaction at the result. The machines, instead of being blotted out, were now being fused into immobility and thus presenting considerable difficulties to the advance of those in the rear. A second inspiration struck him, and he called to Ril to slow down.

He swung his ray across the passage and rendered useless the first rank of the pursuers. As those behind came climbing over them, he swung the ray back along the line so that they were fused above their fellows. Still more came scrambling over, and again the ray swept across. A grim smile of success twitched his mouth as he steadily continued his tactics. At great speed, he was building a solid wall of fused metal between himself and the pursuers. It was but a short time before it blocked the passage from the floor to the curved roof.

The moment it was complete, he jumped to the ground and ran forward to where Jessica's inert form rested in the grip of the feelers. He was thankful that she had been unconscious throughout the rescue. It was the work of a few seconds to strip off the clinging remnants of her captor's tentacles and lift her up to Julian, who had taken his place at the panel opening. Swinging himself hurriedly aboard, he called to Ril for full speed. There was no telling how long the fused wall would hold.

The remaining length of passage was covered without incident, or even sight of other machines, but they emerged into the main traffic artery to find a different state of affairs. They had last seen it almost empty; now, it was crowded. A number of mechanisms rushed at them with antagonistic intent, and were promptly rayed before they reached a dangerous distance. Following them were others; but by no means all the machines in sight were concerned in the attack. The majority continued peacefully to go about their appointed tasks. Either the alarm had not been intended for all, or else it had been cut short before it became general. Whatever the cause, the result was a great jostling and tangling of machines at cross-purposes. The attackers were obstructed and hindered at every turn by the instinctive way in which the others pursued their routine work.

Ril, quick to perceive their advantage in the turmoil of the two inflexible orders, steered to one side and jostled into the stream of outgoing vehicles. The whole procession moved at a steady, uniform speed, and they were swept along with it. The attackers, unable to alter the instinctive march, were left with no course but to follow in their wake at such points as they could contrive to wedge themselves into the moving queue. Roy looked round over the moving ranks and realised that they were safe, barring accidents, until the open should be reached.

Within the metal shell, Julian was doing his best to restore Jessica to consciousness, and looking with anger at the great weals imprinted on her arms and legs. When her abductor was caught, it had evidently closed its grip the more firmly in a determination not to lose its prey, and she had fainted from the constriction. At last her eyes opened, and she looked up at him.

'What's happened?' she asked, attempting to move her stiffened limbs. He explained.

'And Roy?'

At the sound of her voice, Roy withdrew from his observation post and walked forward, in the crouched attitude that the cramped quarters demanded. He took one of her hands in both of his, and gazed down into her smiling face.

'Thank God you're safe, Jessica. Until that thing snatched you away, I didn't realise——'

Jessica's eyes were starry. 'You didn't realise what, Roy?'

'I didn't realise how much I——'

'Heat-rays ready!' interrupted Ril. 'We're nearly out.'

'Oh, damn!' muttered Roy, as he sprang back to his station.

CHAPTER NINE

THE ESCAPE TO THE PAST

IN the open, Ril gave the machine full power and sent it tearing away from the main body. Presently, the pursuers also drew clear and came scudding in swift chase. Roy picked off the leaders with sharp blasts of heat, but every second more and more of the machines pouring out of the mountain entrance were joining the hunting pack. It became no longer a straggling pursuit, but a solid block of shining mechanisms bearing down. Had the way ahead been clear, possibly they could have held their own in the matter of speed, but once in the forest, the superior control and familiarity of the insects with their own machines began to tell. Roy, with a ray tube in each hand, thanked Providence that no ballistic weapons were known to the ants; he had his work cut out to pick off the advancing units.

'Ahead!' cried Ril, and Roy whipped round, to see a line of machines drawn across their path. A quick switch of the ray served to clear the way, but it also sent a patch of trees bursting into flame. Ril held on, and plunged them through the gauntlet of fire.

Something fell across Roy's shoulders and half wrenched him from his perch. He turned to find an insect-machine racing alongside; it had pursued a parallel course behind masking trees, and seized his momentary diversion of attention to cut in on him. He crooked one arm beneath the metal casing-edge, in an effort to resist the pull, but slowly he felt his muscles giving in beneath the relentless tugging. Desperately he wriggled the other arm, in an attempt to bring the ray to bear. He was thankful that it had not occurred to the insects to snatch at the fast-moving legs of the stolen machine...

The pull of the tentacle grew stronger, and he called loudly to the others. He felt a pair of arms clutch his legs. He ached painfully, as the machine tightened its grip. Fingers grasped the ray tube from the arm he had crooked below, and Jessica thrust herself up beside him with the tube in her hand. Quick as thought, the whole bunch of tentacles were shorn from their roots. Then, turning it downward, she fused the front legs. The fore end dropped suddenly, and the attacker pitched back over front in a final, shattering somersault.

Roy disentangled himself from the wrapping feeler and, side by side with Jessica, went to work at clearing away the nearest of the pursuers. The rays flashed in a furious semi-circle, but the encroaching machines were constantly supplemented; it seemed that they must shortly be overcome by sheer, clogging weight of numbers.

'Hold tight, there! We've got to risk this,' called Ril from below. Roy glanced ahead, and saw that they had again reached the river—unfortunately, not at the same shallow spot as they had crossed before. This time, a steep bank must be descended and deeper water negotiated. It would be chancing too much to turn along the bank, for they had no means of telling how far their pursuers were spread out to either side.

The machine slithered down the bank and waded out. The water rose above the leg-sockets, but it did not flow through the universal joints. It rose further—to within inches of the observation holes; then, thankfully, they felt the floor lift up as the stream-bed rose. On the farther bank, Roy called Ril to halt. The machines had not followed them. They had collected in a line, hesitant and unwilling to risk a wetting. It seemed that the fugitives were safe. Then, just as Roy drew a breath of relief, one machine, more intrepid than the rest, came sliding down. Instantly he rayed it; and a burst of steam arose from the water around.

But the necessary lead had been given. A second later, half a dozen or more were slithering into the water. With no compunction, he played his ray upon them. He hoped by example to stop them from making a mass attack, for it would be impossible to check all the hundreds which now lined the bank. But as he vaporised the last of the waders, an interruption occurred. Something came swinging above their heads and landed with a crash on the opposite bank.

'The red stalkers!' cried Jessica. 'They're attacking them. Quickly, Ril, get into the trees! They haven't seen us yet.'

They scuttered from the danger zone. Under cover of the branches, they stopped and looked back. Indescribable confusion was raging among the machines, and at first it was difficult to see the reason. But as they watched, a net of glittering red metal came sailing through the air and fell upon the white machines. Evidently the red stalkers used rocks only against isolated enemies; when they really went into action, they had other weapons. One net followed another, and with every move they made, the white machines became more hopelessly entangled. From being a collection of perfectly controlled units, they soon changed into no more than a writhing mass of a myriad glittering parts, surging frantically this way and that, enmeshing themselves the more as they struggled to escape.

Roy caught a glimpse of the first red biped striding forward, metal nets swinging from its jointed arms.

'Time for us to go,' he said.

Ril threw in the switch, and they scurried away into the green obscurity of the forest.

An unexpected sight greeted them at the cliffs. Del's time-traveller, constructed for safety within the cave, had been brought out and lowered to the ground. The other five members of the party were clustered round it, apparently in conference over some knotty point. One of the Numen let out a cry, as they broke from the trees. Jim Hollis swung round with ready weapon. Roy hailed him loudly, and the other's face broke into a grin. A moment later, the machine came to a halt in the middle of a congratulatory group. The greetings over, Roy asked:

'Why have you brought the traveller down here? Either an ant-machine or a red stalker may come along any minute. One stone landing on that would ruin all your work.'

Del explained. It was necessary that the traveller be some-how conveyed to the cliff-top. A break, less than a mile away, offered ample possibility for men to climb, but the problem of raising the machine appeared hard to solve.

'But why lift it at all? Why not work it here?'

'Look at the cliffs,' said Del.

'Well, what about them?'

'They've been caused by some earth-fault, and are very recent. If we were to work the machine here, we would prob-ably finish in the part of the cliff now fallen away—the result of that, I leave to your imagination.'

Roy looked thoughtful. 'I hadn't thought of that danger,' he admitted.

'Nor did many others—or else they risked it, as we did. Many travellers must have been built in the past. I wonder how many of their unfortunate occupants reached this year at the bottom of new seas, entombed in mountains or even high above ground-level. It is nothing less than miraculous that we few survived.'

Roy gazed dubiously at the cage-work in which all their hopes were centred. His expression cleared; turning to Ril, he asked:

'Couldn't the machine carry it?'

Ril was doubtful. Since the traveller had to contain the whole party, it was far heavier and larger than its forerunners.

'We can try,' he said, with little conviction. Edging their captured ant-machine close, he wound the four tentacles firmly around the traveller, and carefully drew back the lifting lever. The burden lurched slightly, but it did not rise; instead, the white machine tilted forward, its back legs in the air.

'Too heavy in the bows,' Jim Hollis remarked. 'Let's see if we can bring her stern down.'

The combined weights of himself, Roy and the two Numen, perched at the extreme rear, served effectively to change the balance. The traveller was lifted clear of the ground. Very cautiously and slowly, Ril set the legs in motion, and the machine, with its load, moved unsteadily forward.

Progress to the break in the line of cliffs was slow, but slower still was the tedious climb to the top. Again and again it was necessary to assist the slipping legs of the machine, and to give purchase to scrambling metal claws. Nevertheless, their ad-miration for the adaptability of the machine rose as it over-came successive obstacles, forging patiently and relentlessly up the rough way. All nine of the castaways became increasingly jubilant as the top was neared, even the two Numen being caught up in the prevailing high spirits, and wearing grins of pleasure.

As they scrambled at last over the skyline, Roy looked back in triumph at the way they had come. But the sight which met him sent the joy from his face. He called out, and pointed below. Ant-machines were scuttling from the trees in a silver stream, racing for the gap.

A few yards more, and they were upon level ground where the traveller could be set down. Assured of its safety, Roy and Jim leaped down and ran back to the brink to meet the attack. Already the leaders were half-way up the rough scramble, before a fanning of rays sent them tumbling back on their fellows. Unencumbered as they were, they could climb with astonishing agility; and, as ever, they seemed careless of their casualties. Once the first rush was checked, it became an easy matter for the two men to hold them back. Jim Hollis made a grimace of distaste.

'How long do we keep this up?' he asked. 'It's nothing but a slaughter, even if they are only insects.'

Roy glanced back over his shoulder. He could see that Del was already in the traveller, intently setting his controls.

'Not long, now. Just until Del gets it all fixed,' he returned.

An alarmed cry broke from Jessica. She was pointing along the cliff-edge, where five red stalkers were advancing with deliberate strides. Roy gasped, for he could see that their jointed arms held nets, ready for use. He heard Ril call to him, and saw that the dwarf was manoeuvring the captured ant-craft to face the new danger.

'Your ray tube!' Ril cried, as Roy joined him. 'Hold it up in front!'

Wonderingly, he obeyed. Ril wrapped a tentacle about the tube and set the appendage swaying slowly from left to right. A red metal net came flying towards them. It fell only a few yards short. Ril flicked over the lever which would set the machine marching towards the red stalkers. Then he jumped clear. Roy caught him as he fell, and together they ran for the time traveller.

The entrance snapped to, and through the trellised sides of the cage, Roy took his last sight of the fantastic world. In front, a swarm of silver machines had reached the cliff-top and was pouring over the edge. Away to the right marched their capture, mechanically raying at the red giants. One had already fallen, to go hurtling below; but even as the leg was shorn from another, a metal net settled about the lone attacker.

A glimpse he had of another red net, sailing through the air towards themselves. Then Del pushed over the switch....

Roy and Jessica stood in the darkness. Beside them was the traveller. Of the original nine, it now contained only two. Ril and Kal had been returned to the year 10,424, and with them had stayed the two Numen. Julian had regained his world of 3920, and now they rested at 2200.

'You're determined not to stay?' Roy asked Jim Hollis.

'I am. Twentieth century is where I belong, even if it is a bit over-civilised for me. Say,' he added, 'I wonder what they're goin' to say back there, when I spin 'em this yarn?'

'They won't believe you.'

'Maybe not, but I'll try it.'

The final farewells were exchanged. The entrance closed, and Del set off to deliver his last passenger before he returned to his own future age. Before the eyes of the two, the cage blurred and then, suddenly, was not. A green streak cut the sky.

'That means we're home,' said Jessica. 'It was the Asia-bound rocket.'

'Home,' Roy echoed.

'And we'll never leave it again?'

'Never again!' Roy meant the words as he said them. But somewhere at the back of his mind was a hankering, and that hankering would grow.... What civilisation, for instance, had preceded the ants? What manner of creatures drove the red stalkers? And, above all, what had happened to mankind?

DERELICT OF SPACE

INTRODUCTION

EVEN those too young to remember the Belford affair can scarcely fail to have heard of it, if only through the legend of Captain Belford's treasure hidden somewhere on the Moon. There can be few boys who have not read how Belford and a companion overpowered their police guard in the car that was taking them to prison nearly 60 years ago. And how, dressed in the uniforms of their captors, they bluffed the authorities at an airport and stole a racing rocket-ship from under the official noses.

Everyone who has heard the tale must have wondered what happened to the two who vanished from human knowledge in that ship, as well as about the treasure said to be on the Moon.

Now comes Captain Fearon's explanation. It was he who was the other man in that exploit. For reasons which will be obvious, he withheld publication until after his death, though the account which follows was dictated by him to our representative some six years ago. We have checked much of the story and are fully satisfied that Captain Fearon was actually that same Fearon associated with Captain Belford.

The account which follows was signed and sworn by him, and the original is still in our possession.

CHAPTER ONE

ON PASSAGE TO JUPITER

IT all happened a long time ago. I'm eighty-three now: I was twenty-five then. But, although a lot of things get forgotten, Belford and I seem to have been remembered—though the funny thing is that we're remembered all wrong.

It's queer to live and hear yourself grow into a legend, getting a bit different and a bit more untrue all the time. And I've got a mind to clear things up a bit before I die. If only it stops people going to the Moon and making fools of themselves over the 'Belford Treasure' it'll be something.

The world was different when I first went to space—mind you, I'm not saying it was better or worse but, looking back on it, it seems to have been a whole lot simpler.

I was twenty-four when I got a berth as Second Officer under Captain Belford on the old *Dido*. And right now I'll tell you there wasn't a better man sailing the system; whatever they said about him afterwards. They didn't know him, most of 'em; I did. And when you've been a year in a space-ship with a man there's not much you don't know about him. What happened to him was just a bit of bad luck, such as might have happened to any man on the same job.

He was a big man, such as you don't often find in space-ships; well over six foot, big shouldered, strong as a couple of the rest of us; but he was worth his extra weight, every ounce of it, and in spite of it he could move as fast and sure as a cat. He'd a record as clean as a baby's. If he hadn't he'd not have been there because it cost the Company a pretty penny getting space-suits and suchlike specially made for him.

The Company was the R.R.R.; gone long ago now but in those days it meant something—Red Ribbon Rocketlines—and the *Dido* was a queer old tub that wouldn't even get a spaceworthiness certificate nowadays. She wasn't on the regular lines, never had been. She was built as a salvage ship, and handy for the job she was. In those days nearly all the regular rocket lines ran salvage ships. It was a profitable sideline, not only for getting your own ships out of trouble, but because there were plenty of wrecks drifting about. Ships weren't safe the way they are now. All manner of things could happen to them and, apart from the danger to liners, it wasn't sense to leave valuable ships and cargoes hanging around out there if there was any way of getting them back.

Of course, there wasn't the organisation about it that there is today. That didn't happen till the Dutch got their salvage and towing service fixed—funny, isn't it, how they developed the best space tugs, just as they did the best sea-going tugs?—but there was a lot of work done, a Central Salvage Register Office and all that. Trouble was rivalry between the lines. If we'd only co-operated then, maybe the Dutchmen would never have got a look in.

Well, I was telling you about the old *Dido*. I don't know why she was called *Dido* 'cept that the line named all its ships after women and would have them end in 'o,' which made the choice pretty narrow when you come to think of it—perhaps that's why they went out of business a few years later; couldn't find any more women ending in 'o,' so couldn't have any more ships. Anyway, she was a forty-eight tube ship, less than half the size of a modern Dutch tug, carrying eleven of us all told, well found and, for those days, not too tricky to handle. At least Captain Belford could handle her as well as they manage nowadays with all their modern improvements.

The First Officer was a man called Sinderton. He was a silent sort of chap but good at his job. The crew of eight were all experienced men—there was no room for greenhorns on a salvage ship.

The trip when the trouble occurred started as usual. We took off from the Caledonian Rocket Yard and called in at the Moon to refuel, the same way the tugs do nowadays—a tug, you know, still can't carry enough fuel to get her away from Earth and do her job in space without replenishing somewhere.

When that was done we set out on a course which paralleled but lay to one side of the traffic lane to Jupiter—or rather to the moons of Jupiter, for no one had at that time made a successful landing on the giant himself.

Life on a salvage ship consisted, and probably still does, of spells of complete inaction and rushes of exacting work with no telling how long each is likely to last. It was one of the harder things to get used to and one of the main reasons why a seasoned crew was necessary.

This time we began placidly enough. For over two weeks (Earth-time) we coasted along with the rocket tubes shut off; just being on hand if anyone should need us. But it seemed that nobody did. At regular intervals we would call up all our ships on the Company's lightband wave and ask how things were, and all of them would give us an okay. We began to wish something would happen—and when it did we should wish we had been left in peace. That's the way of it. But just at present nobody was burning out tubes, developing air leaks, getting holed by meteorites or doing any of the hundred and one inconvenient things they so often did do.

It was not until the sixteenth reckoned day that we got a message which started our tubes roaring again and sent us scurrying across space. The liner *Sappho*, homeward bound from Ganymede with a cargo of high-yield pitchblende had sighted a presumed derelict. It was a good, clear direction, giving the positioning of the derelict at the time and her speed and direction, with confidence. We acknowledged, altered course and started up in a few minutes.

Time meant a lot on such jobs. We had got to reach the derelict before anyone else spotted her. The ruling was that salvage rights could be claimed by the first ship to establish contact with the wreck. Immediately that was done, the office back on Earth was informed, the claim was then checked and registered, and an announcement of its validity broadcast. The principle seemed fair enough, though more than once two or even three salvage ships informed of the chance at more or less the same time had pelted across space, half-killing their crews with acceleration in their efforts to make the claim. On this occasion there was no one else in on it so far as we knew, but it was always risky to waste time.

Two days later, close on the position we had calculated the wreck to have reached, we were decelerating as violently as we had speeded up. Captain Belford was at the controls while the First Officer and I were swivelling telescopes from one point of light to another, desperately searching the star-pricked blackness for the one little gleam which was a rocket-ship. Of course, that was no way to find her, but there was just the several-millions-to-one chance that we might catch a glimpse of her: it is said to have been done once or twice.

Belford called Sinderton away from his telescope and handed over the controls to him. While we were still decelerating he set up the sensitive screens ready for use when we should come to a stop. On the screens, as you probably know, moving bodies trace lines of light and though all the bodies in the heavens are moving, those which are closest appear to travel fastest. In our position there could be nothing nearer than the derelict—except the unlikely presence of a second derelict—so that it was necessary for us to scan each section of space for the fastest moving line of light. If we could find it among the rest—no easy task in itself—we should have found the ship. Well, we did: it took us a good twelve hours of screen studying before we located her, but that wasn't bad. It might easily have taken three days or more. I've known it do that.

CHAPTER TWO

WRECK OF A TREASURE SHIP

As soon as we'd made certain of the derelict we turned and steadied the *Dido* on her side tubes, then one brief burst on the main propeller tubes was enough to send us sliding in her direction. As we closed, another short burst on the forward rockets brought us to rest within a couple of hundred yards of her. (When I say 'brought us to rest' I use the term figuratively, of course, to mean that we and she were travelling in the same direction at the same speed.)

Captain Belford picked up his telephone and spoke to two men already wearing space-suits and waiting in the air-lock.

'All right. Let 'em go,' he said.

We watched from the windows as the men heaved out an electro-magnet. We couldn't see the men, of course, but we saw the magnet float out slowly and deliberately with its leads and cable looping behind it in slow-motion. A few seconds later another followed it. The Captain waited, hands on two rheostats, until they were over half-way to the wreck.

'Make connection and stand by,' he told the radio operator, then he turned the knob.

It's a fascinating thing to watch coupling-magnets come to life, so to speak. One moment they are drifting idly along, the next they appear to awake and suddenly discover a purpose. They veer a little and surge gently forward towards the nearest mass of metal while the looping lines which hold them gradually straighten out. The Captain gave them a minute's power to pull them towards the derelict, and then shut off and waited. As the first magnet made gentle contact with the hull he switched on again and it glued itself to the metal side. A moment later the second magnet gripped.

'Make the claim,' he told the operator.

Two space-suited figures left our ship, pulling themselves along the magnet cables to the other at great speed. The Captain took up a micro-wave headset and listened. One of the men in space-suits reached the wreck and pushed himself off the magnet so that he floated round to her bow.

'*Excelsis*,' said the Captain suddenly. 'Tell the Register Office.'

'Aye, aye, sir,' acknowledged the operator.

'Haul in,' ordered the Captain, putting down the micro wave set.

A small motor began to whirr and the cables between the two ships started to tighten.

'Cut,' said Captain Belford as we started to drift together.

We waited while the two ships slowly approached one another.

It began to be possible to get a better idea of the *Excelsis*'s size. The proportion of our space-suited men against her had told us she was big, but we did not fully realise how big until we came closer alongside. She'd have made ten of the old *Dido*.

'*Excelsis*, that'll be a Three Star ship,' murmured the Captain. 'I seem to remember something about her, but I can't recall it at the moment.'

'Third of three sister ships on the Three Star service, sir,' said the First Officer. 'Supposed to be the last word in safety in their day. She and the *Isis* were both lost. The other, the *Artemis*, was broken up several years ago. I'm afraid I can't remember anything else offhand. It'll be in the book, sir.'

'Never mind, we'll know soon enough.'

A minute or two later the operator announced:

'Claim of Captain Belford of the *Dido*, to salvage of *Excelsis*, Captain Whitter, registered and approved subject to confirmation. Work may proceed. *Excelsis*, 250 tubes, lost in space 12 years ago, homeward bound from Ganymede. Reported serious damage to propeller tubes. Unnavigable. Search vessels unable to find her. 60 passengers. 20 officers and crew, mixed cargo. Gold, patchatal oil, tillfer fibre, ganywood, 3 bags of mail. Property of Plume Line, successors to Three Star Line, yards at Lough Swilly, Ireland.'

The Captain looked half-elated, half-dubious as he listened to the radio operator's message. If the cargo mentioned was in any quantity it looked as if we should net something like a record salvage payment—if we could get it home.

'Gold,' he muttered, 'and ganywood. The two heaviest things they could find. There's some sense in ganywood, at least it's useful. But gold, what's the good of that? You can't use it for anything.'

'Except money,' I said.

He looked at me contemptuously.

'Nobody's used gold as money for God knows how long. You never see it except in jewellery. It's pretty near useless, and yet they're forever digging it out of mines all over the system. And what for? Just to take it to Earth and bury it somewhere where no one ever sees it. Then they all look bright and pleased and say their credit's gone up. Damned nonsense, I call it. Trying to get gold from one planet to another has cost more lives and money than anything else in spacework.'

'And yet,' said I, 'if everybody wants it, that means it has a value.'

'Fictitious value,' he snorted.

'Fictitious or not, it'll mean a lot to you and to us if we get it back all right,' I said.

'Maybe, but I still say it's not worth the fuss they make about it. It might as well be lying about out there,'—he pointed to the starry blackness beyond the window—'just floating around in space as locked up in a vault on Earth. If I had my way that's where it would be, and a lot of good space sailors who are going to lose their lives handling it would keep them. There's some heavy stuff you've got to handle, but it's not gold.'

All the time he was talking the two ships were slowly coming together. I was paying more attention to them than I was to the Captain. The 'gold menace' was one of his hobby-horses. I'd heard it all before and a lot more. And however he felt about it the fact remained that he'd do his damnedest to get it safely to Earth and we should all be rewarded for assisting him.

As the two ships gently touched he resumed his official manner.

'Mr. Fearon, you will attend to the grappling and conduct a preliminary survey of the ship, please.'

'Aye, aye, sir,' I said.

I had put on my space-suit in readiness. It did not take long to add the helmet and with two of the crew I passed out of the air-lock.

We three, with the help of the two men already on the *Excelsis*, manoeuvred with cables until we had brought the two locks conveniently close, and then made fast. I reported over the micro-wave, there came a gentle flare from the *Dido*'s stern tubes, and as the two ships started to move we turned our attention to examining our capture.

I find that Worldsmen often find it difficult to grasp space conditions, so it may help if I explain a little.

It must be understood that a derelict in space is never stationary. Very often she is travelling at a considerable speed and quite possibly in an altogether different direction from the one the salvage ship intends her to take. The first thing to be done after making fast is therefore to ease her gently on to the right course, for it is easy to see that as long as she is allowed to continue on her own, time which cannot be made up is being wasted.

It is a ticklish bit of work this, for, however strong your steel coupling hawsers, the strain must come on them gradually and not too intensely at any time. Set on the right course the tug begins to apply a cautious acceleration, perhaps of not more than a few feet per second, if a big ship is in tow. This means time is being saved, but causes no inconvenience to men working on the derelict. In space there is no subjective difference between travelling at seven miles a second or at one mile an hour; acceleration is what you feel and an increase of a few feet per second is negligible in practice.

The only risk is of a man losing his hold and being left behind, and that is slight; for one thing he should be using a life-line, but even if he is not, the recoil from a shot or two with a hand pistol should easily enable him to catch up.

When we saw the rockets start, all five of us clipped life-lines to our belts and began our preliminary survey, reporting back on the micro-wave as we went.

It was clear enough pretty quickly what had happened. Something had struck the *Excelsis*'s tail, carrying away three quarters of her tubes and mangling the rest. The stern was just a mess but the rest of her seemed intact. I heard the Captain grunt as I reported, and though he made no comment I knew what he was thinking.

It was going to be a nasty business. It is better, far, far better to find a derelict which has been finished off quickly. When a meteorite has knocked away part of the habitable quarters, or when it has gone right through and the air has rushed out, you know it was all over quickly. Death is never too good to look at, though if it's sudden it's usually pretty clean. But when the living quarters are undamaged and the people in them have had to wait and see death come slowly, you'll find that some pretty horrible things have happened before the end. I could tell you some things—but I shan't: I don't care to think of them even now.

'Have to cut into her?' the Captain asked.

'Yes, sir.'

'All right. I'll put the stuff out.'

Cutting into a ship is a tedious business. First you attach a large metal cup to the side and weld it on all round the edges and it looks as if the ship had developed a boil. Then a man gets into the cup by a small door in the top of it.

A cutter is handed in after him. He shuts the door from his side, for it's made to resist outward and not inward pressure, and gets to work with the cutter. The object of the cup is, of course, to prevent the escape of any air.

First, the man cuts away a circle of the outer hull, making a hole large enough for him to crawl through. If he is satisfied that the inner hull is intact, he re-opens the door of the cup and gets rid of the circle he has cut by pushing it outside. Then, after shutting the door again, he turns his attention to the inner hull. He trains his cutter steadily on a single point and watches carefully.

This is the part of the job which needs most judgment. The moment the area under the flame of his cutter begins to bulge, he switches off. His object is to let the air come as gently as possible into the evacuated space between the inner and outer hulls. If he lets it come with a rush he may have an extremely unpleasant time of it. More than that, if it so happens that the welding-on of the cup was imperfect, he and it may be shot off into space and the air from the wreck irretrievably lost.

Therefore, he makes the smallest hole he can and keeps a careful watch on his pressure gauge as the air comes through. Not until the needle has ceased to move can he go any further. When that has happened, however, and the pressure in his cup ceases to rise, he cuts a circle through the inner hull as he did through the outer, and at last he is able to get into the ship. Straightaway he reports and makes his way to the air-lock. There he gets ready to operate the lever which opens the outer door.

It would, of course, be much simpler if someone could devise a satisfactory method of opening the outer door from outside, but for several reasons—the main one being the super-heating of outer shell in an atmosphere—no reliable mechanism has yet been made.

CHAPTER THREE

SALVAGE IN SPACE

WITH the *Excelsis*, it took several hours' work before the cutter-in was able to report that we could come aboard.

'All right. Open up,' Captain Belford directed.

The rest of us who had retired on board the *Dido* to wait looked at him expectantly. He chose the boarding party and we hurried into our suits. While we dressed he talked to the man on the other ship.

'How is it?'

'Pretty grim, sir.'

We were all wearing micro-wave sets in preparation for the job, and we could follow both sides of the conversation.

'Air pressure?' asked the Captain.

'Thirteen point seven pounds, sir. Seems to have held it perfectly. Releasing it into the double hull seems just about to account for the drop from normal.'

'Breathable?'

'Pretty bad, sir, by the look of things. I didn't risk trying.'

'Don't then. Got the lock open yet?'

'Yes, sir.'

'All right. We're coming now.'

From our own lock we pushed off and floated across to the open door of the other. We took little with us but welding arcs and some batteries to start up the air purifiers.

I'm not going to tell you what the *Excelsis* was like inside; it's not decent to try. All I'll say is that some of the passengers and crew had contrived to last a pretty long time. I felt pretty green and wondered if I was going to be sick. I had to take a hold on myself: being sick in a space-suit's a dangerous as well as an unpleasant business.

I was detailed, with the help of one of the hands, to weld up the recently made cut and to pump the air back from between the hulls. I think both of us were pretty glad to leave the clearing up operations to the rest.

Since space travel began it has been the practice to leave its victims out in space. And in my opinion it is a good thing, too. Certainly it could be no consolation to relatives to see the poor things which have to be thrust out of a wreck's air-lock to drift slowly astern. And that's another reason for keeping up some acceleration while salvage work is going on. If you don't, you can't lose those bodies. They just keep on drifting round, gravitating gradually to the mass of the ship. It's bad for the nerves to see dead men floating past the windows all the time.

When we'd finished our welding and pumping we found that the rest were nearly through with the nastiest part of the job.

The man in charge of the disposal squad was reporting tonelessly to the Captain who had been conducting a detailed examination of cargo and stores.

'Thirty complete bodies, sir. Seventeen of those identified. Here's the list of them, sir.'

Captain Belford held out his hand and took it slowly. No one spoke for a minute or more. Only thirty complete bodies

—and there had been eighty passengers and crew....

The Captain carefully put the list away in a pocket. Then he stepped over to a window and stood a moment looking at a thousand suns flaring in their bed of black. I felt he was trying to see them in all their pitilessness as the men on the *Excelsis* had seen them. His space-suit made a grotesque giant of him. Then with a scarcely audible sigh, he began to recite the prayer for those who have died in space.

The clearing up of the *Excelsis* was regular routine work. Only two of her fuel tanks had leaked, and the first thing we did was to fill our own from those which hadn't leaked—it's axiomatic to fill your tanks when you can in space. You never know when you are going to need just that extra bit of power.

There was a little food, just a few unopened tins of biscuits. The poor devils had made the food last longer than the water, for those tanks were dry to the last drop. The gold was intact in the strong room; we checked it over. The ganywood was still safely clamped down in the hold. One of the drums of patchatal oil had been broken open—we reckoned some poor thirst-crazy chap had tried to drink it. The rest were intact, and so were the bales of tillfer fibre.

The personal belongings we left in the cabins where we found them, just fastening any loose things down for safety. When we got the ship in, someone would go through them with the passenger list and return them to the next of kin.

All that is the lighter part of salvage work. A bit depressing, of course, but easy because once the air purifiers have got going you can dispense with space-suits.

Next came the outside work, and the first thing was to get a wide mesh net round the part of the ship we were going to work on. You can't cling on to the polished hull and you must have something to give you purchase when you're handling tools, so the answer is the net. You can climb about on it and hook yourself into it when necessary. When we'd got that fixed we began fixing ringbolts in the side.

It's a tedious job, but it has to be done and it has to be done well. There's only one way of easing the fall of a derelict or a ship out of control—that is by use of parachutes. And the attachment of parachutes is going to depend in the last stage upon the firm fixing of those ring-bolts. The strength of the parachutes' fabric, the braking effect of their area, the tensile strength of their steel hawsers; all that can be worked out mathematically on paper, but the fixing of the bolts is different; it must be trusted to the skill, care and conscientious workmanship of the men doing the job. There must be no botching or covering up of bad work. Luckily, it's a job that seldom has to be hurried.

The *Excelsis* was a big ship. To make as sure of her as possible we were going to attach every parachute we carried and that meant a lot of work. Nevertheless we had more than three-quarters of the bolts in place before we began to decelerate. That meant we'd plenty of time, for our rate of deceleration was the same as our acceleration and would therefore take longer. We had to lose, you see, not only the speed we had worked up, but also the speed the wreck was travelling when we found her, in order to ease her close to Earth at as slow a rate as possible. It meant several weeks of slowing up.

It's no good my being too technical, but I must give you some idea of the ticklish job it is to land a wreck successfully. There are a hundred things which can go wrong. Dozens of calculations to make, and a slip in any of them is likely to mean failure.

The first stage is to attain a state of equilibrium between the Earth and the Moon where one is stationary—again I speak relatively as one must do in space, actually one is moving round the Earth, but at a constant distance from it. There the final preparations for descent are made.

The salvage ship again refills her fuel tanks and any surplus fuel from the derelict is jettisoned for safety. Much wreckage has already been cut away in the first clearing up, now the empty fuel tanks are cut out and set adrift with an impulse in the direction of the Moon. The hulk is made as light as possible for it is intended to drop her in the sea and it is hoped that she may float. We had little hope of the *Excelsis* floating, seeing the weight of gold and ganywood she carried, but on general principles we saw to it that she was as light as she could be.

Then the ship is sealed up, the main coupling hawsers which have bound the two together are cast off leaving only the magnets and their hawsers as links, and the parachutes are made fast to the ring-bolts. The practical work for the crew is finished; the rest depends upon the captain's calculations and his consequent manoeuvres. He and the first officer get down to figuring and checking one another's results.

This is no light work. The captain knows the approximate spot where he intends to drop the derelict and he has got to get her into such a position that she will fall there or thereabouts. He knows the load his magnets will hold and that, with his estimated weight of his salvage, tells him how much pull and steerage effect he will be able to exert. He must work out the balancing of forces—the pull of the Moon, of the Sun, of the Earth, and the rotation of the spot he aims at, relatively to the Moon. Everything which can be used to slow or shorten the final descent must be employed. Finally, he must find out by radio as much as he can about weather conditions on Earth and make allowance for them at the last possible moment.

In general, we were feeling that we were near the end of a profitable and not too onerous piece of work. From the salvagers' point of view the *Excelsis* was as straightforward a job as one could hope for, except for the heavy cargo. It simplifies tasks a great deal when the air has been held; you don't have to build new pieces of double wall or fit automatically-closing valves to take in air as she drops.

Seeing that the Plume Line yards were in North Ireland, Captain Belford aimed to drop her a bit out in the Atlantic and make it a short tow by sea. He informed the Salvage Register Office that he was aiming at the neighbourhood of 51° North by 12° West and received their approval. He and the First Officer verified the chronometer's reading and went ahead with the calculations. They checked and re-checked one another's figures with care before they announced to us the exact minute of action.

With some eight hours to go before that time came we all turned in for a while.

CHAPTER FOUR

FALL OF THE *EXCELSIS*

HALF an hour before we were due to start, Captain Belford had already fastened himself into his chair and was firing short bursts on the side tubes to obtain the right inclination. We all strapped on our safety-belts and waited, watching the minute-hand on the chronometer.

On the correct second the *Dido* began to throb gently as her tubes fired. We felt a slight tug a moment later as the hawsers on the magnets took up. We moved gradually Earthward. Behind us came the *Excelsis*, started on her long last fall.

The First Officer and I were making continuous observations, reporting our angles and distances to the Captain. He verified them on a table he had drawn up and pinned on a board in front of him, correcting the slightest deviation from his planned time-course by a short burst on one or another of the bunches of rocket tubes.

This manoeuvre, known technically as a 'linked fall,' would go on for a long time yet. It should last, in fact, until we were within four or five thousand miles of the Earth's surface when we would cast off and look to our landing while the *Excelsis* fell free.

But all the first part was a time of constant watch and correction. We were falling together, but the *Dido*'s was no dead fall. All the time she was moving laterally, now this way and now that, tugging and altering the course of the larger vessel, trimming her to hit a calculated spot on the surface of Earth which grew all the time larger and nearer. As delicate a job as any there is, for the disabled ship must be urged to one side or another with the utmost nicety and precision; there must be no jerks or sudden bursts of power which might detach the magnets from her hull. Their hold was the limiting factor of our power over her, but used by an expert it was enough.

The radio operator looked up quickly and reported.

'North-westerly wind rising rapidly to gale force, west of Ireland, sir,' he said.

Captain Belford, hunched in front of his chart, grunted.

'Tell them I'll try to compensate.' He altered the position of some of his controls, muttering more to himself than us: 'Gale, and they gave it as twenty-four hours fair prospect. I suppose they'll learn something about weather, one day.'

He steered the *Dido* round to the other side of the *Excelsis* and in that moment the thing, which was to spoil the rest of his life, happened.

He fired on his tail rockets and I say it now, again, as I said it in evidence before, no man could have handled them with better judgment. There was no jerk. I was looking out of the window directly facing the *Excelsis* and I saw the magnet float away from her side. To this day I cannot say why—it may be that the cable kinked and broke, that there was a short somewhere; I can't tell, but I know that that magnet was loose before our cable to the other magnet drew taut.

Instinctively and instantaneously I shouted a warning, but it came too late. Captain Belford's judgment had been based on the hold of two magnets. Before he had time to reach the controls the second magnet had pulled off and came skimming towards us as though the wire rope which held it had been elastic.

I had never known the Captain to lose his head, and he kept

it now. A burst on the side tubes jumped us out of the way, so that the heavy magnet just missed us and went past with its 200 yards of cable looping behind it.

'Cast off,' he ordered.

A man leaned over and pulled a switch. An automatic jaw severed the cable and the magnet sped away into space with the rope curling like a slowly moving snake behind it.

It was a nasty half-minute. That second magnet had sprung back at us with a force which might have holed us if it had hit: at best, we should have got some nasty dents. With that danger past we looked again at the *Excelsis*.

The distance between us had widened and she was falling free. I saw Captain Belford frown, but there was only one possible decision. Even had it been possible to close with her we should not have time to manoeuvre her after the delay of recoupling. The course he took, and to my mind the only useful course, was to check our own fall and to hope for the best as far as she was concerned. There was nothing to be gained by running the risk of losing both ships.

He made up his mind in a few seconds. First, he cut free the other magnet, then a touch of the side tubes turned our stern to Earth, and the main rockets began to fire. It felt as if strong brakes had suddenly been applied. The *Excelsis* with her un-opened parachutes tied about her in bundles, seemed to shoot down from our level towards the growing Earth beneath. She dwindled to a silver shell, a shining bullet, a point of light and then suddenly was gone.

The Captain spoke to the radio operator.

'Inform the Salvage Register Office that the *Excelsis* has been lost and is now in free fall. Confirm that her intended descent was to be at 51° North, 12° West and that it is not possible at this distance to predict her degree of deviation.

'Get the weather report from the Caledonian Yard and tell them that we are coming in.'

And that's the plain truth about the *Excelsis*. That and nothing more. A simple accident and not a Machiavellian scheme. Things like that are bound to happen from time to time, and they may happen to anyone. Sometimes no harm is done, at others the wreck may be lost altogether, and then the captain of the salvage ship will have to account for all his actions before the regular official board of inquiry. There is no doubt that had such a routine investigation taken place Captain Belford would have been exonerated from all blame by a body of men as conversant with the hazards of space as he himself. Instead, he was called upon to face fantastic accusations thrown at him by men who were grossly ignorant of the possibilities and impossibilities of spacemanship.

The first hint of the trouble occurred about an hour after we had landed.

We were in the Yard clubroom drinking a welcome whisky while officials went over the *Dido*. It was always a tedious wait. Before we could get the all-clear and be allowed to go our ways, the Excise men had to search the ship for dutiable goods, the police for prohibited articles, and the Company's officers had to check up on equipment, stores, fuel and so on.

We were glad enough to be back, but we didn't talk a lot. The main question for all of us was whether we should see any return for our work on the *Excelsis*, or whether she was utterly lost and our salvage money with her. The Captain, with the weight of responsibility upon him, stared gloomily into his glass most of the time, and, except when it needed refilling, seldom opened his mouth to speak.

We had been there close on a couple of hours and were beginning to feel that our clearance papers were about due when the door opened and the head of the Caledonian Rocket Yard Police came in. We all looked at him hopefully. Inspector Macraig was as popular with spacemen as any policeman was likely to be. He was a man of integrity, a stickler for the spirit of the law, but no fusser about its letter. He'd done spacework himself and he knew how it felt. This time, however, he did not give us his usual cheery greeting. He was frowning slightly and there was a troubled look in his eyes. He nodded abstractedly to the rest of us and made his way straight to Captain Belford. At his expression, the Captain checked his natural invitation to a drink and waited.

'William Belford, Wilfred Sinderton, James Fearon,' he said, 'it is my duty to place you under arrest.'

No one spoke for a moment. My own first reaction, and the First Officer's too, he told me afterwards, was to wonder which of us on the *Dido* had been smuggling or running dope—and how it had been done, for on that trip we had called nowhere but at the Moon, and there's precious little chance of getting hold of prohibited drugs or anything else there.

The Captain looked stunned for a moment, then he rose to his feet, overtopping the inspector by a good nine inches.

'And the charge?' he asked.

'Criminal negligence,' said the Inspector quietly.

His expression changed as he looked into the Captain's incredulous face.

'I'm sorry, Belford. Direct 'phone orders from London.'

'Negligence of what?' the Captain demanded.

'They didn't say. No details were given officially.'

'But unofficially?'

'Well, information has just been received here that the *Excelsis* came down somewhere in Germany and blew half a town to hell.'

We all stared at him.

'But that's impossible,' I broke in.

'Absurd,' said Sinderton. 'Why I supervised the cutting away of her tanks myself. There wasn't an ounce of explosive on her.'

We both looked at the Captain.

'There's a mistake somewhere,' he said. 'I made an inspection of the ship with Mr. Sinderton and Mr. Fearon. All fuel that had not been taken on to the *Dido* was jettisoned.'

The Inspector looked unhappy.

'I know you, and I know that there must be a mistake. But my orders were clear. I am to send you to London under arrest as soon as possible. I'm sorry.'

'It's not your fault, Macraig, of course. There's some official muddle somewhere. The sooner we can get to London and clear it up, the better for everyone. When can we start?'

'At once, I imagine. I told them to get a rocket-'plane ready. It ought to be waiting by now.'

'All right.' The Captain tipped down the last of his whisky. 'Let's go,' he added, and led the way purposefully to the door.

CHAPTER FIVE

DISASTER EXTRAORDINARY

WE could not tell what had happened to cause the misunderstanding, but all of us suspected mere exaggeration. It was possible that the ship had disintegrated as it hit: in that case hurried reports might easily have represented a severe impact as an explosion. There would be no difficulty, we thought, in clearing ourselves of an explosion charge; every man of the *Dido*'s company would testify that the wreck had been cleared out of fuel to the last ounce. There might be a charge of inefficiency in fixing the cables, but we all had good records for workmanship and every incentive to bring the *Excelsis* down safely if we could.

We made the trip to London less in a state of worry than of irritation at misrepresentation.

An official police-car was waiting for us on King's Cross landing-roof and in it we were carried swiftly to Scotland Yard. Inside the building we were conducted without delay to the office of the Deputy Assitant Commissioner of the Special Branch. We did not know which he was at first, for three men apparently of equal rank awaited us. The manner in which they received us was curious, it seemed an odd blend of formality and sympathy. Certainly, it did not suggest that they considered us to be criminally negligent.

First, we received the customary warning. They wished to question us, but we were legally within our rights in refusing to answer.

Captain Belford waved that aside. He had a clear conscience and was willing to give all the help he could. He was sure he could say the same for his two officers. We agreed and settled down to answer a series of questions.

Were we sure all the explosive had been jettisoned? Might there not have been some other kind of explosive concealed among the tillfer fibre or in the stacked ganywood? How many ringbolts and parachutes had we attached? Just how had we come to lose the *Excelsis*? How much gold was there on board of her?

The men knew their job. Their questions were apposite and exhaustive. It went on for quite a time. We answered all we could and they seemed satisfied with our replies.

The Captain told them all they asked and kept to the point. Not until they appeared to have finished did he put a question of his own.

'Can't you tell us something about it?' he said. 'We've only heard that the *Excelsis* fell and did damage somewhere in Germany.'

For answer one of the interrogators picked up a newspaper which had recently been brought in and handed it to him. The First Officer and I got up and read it over his shoulder. The headline was right across the page:

'ROCKET SHIP WRECKS TOWN'

There followed a short but lurid account. It needed only half an eye to see that it had been hurriedly written up from very scanty information.

We learned that the disaster had occurred in Pfaffheim,

Würtemburg, shortly before 12.30 p.m. (11.30 a.m. G.M.T.). A series of colossal explosions had occurred, rocking the whole town, shattering a number of buildings and causing the collapse of many more. So great had been the detonation that it had startled citizens in Stuttgart, 40 miles away. No figures of the dead and injured were yet available, but it was feared that they would run into thousands. The loss of life might have been greater but for the fact that most workers had left the factories for their mid-day meal.

Numerous witnesses had testified to seeing a rocket ship unbraked by any parachutes falling rapidly into the town immediately before the explosions occurred. Inquiries at the Salvage Register Office revealed that only one ship was known to be approaching Earth in a free fall, the *Excelsis*. It was unlikely, in the extreme, that there could be another.

We read the sketchy and unsatisfactory account rapidly. I don't think any of us doubted for a moment that it was the *Excelsis*. The Central Office would have been sure to know of another ship in a similar condition, for it is in every salvage ship's interest to register her claim to a wreck as soon as possible. But, for all that, we did not clearly understand the account.

'A *series* of explosions?' asked the Captain, looking up at the three officials. 'What do they mean by that? If there had been explosives on her she'd have gone up in one mighty bang.'

'Where is Pfaffheim?' asked Sinderton, before the others could answer. 'I thought I knew Würtemburg fairly well, but I've never heard of the place.'

'Our own official notification from Germany speaks of one explosion, not a series,' said the man who had given us the newspaper. 'As for Pfaffheim——' He reached for a gazetteer, found the right page and pushed it across the desk.

He watched us with raised eyebrows as we read:

Pfaffheim: Village, Würtemburg, river Jagar, 30 miles S.E. Stuttgart, pop. 2,100. Agricultural.

'There seem,' I said, 'to be some differences of opinion here. One explosion, not a series, 30 miles from Stuttgart, not 40, thousands of casualties in a population of 2,100, among factory workers in an agricultural district.'

I looked at the date on the gazetteer. It was current all right.

'Well?' I asked.

Our leading questioner shrugged his shoulders.

'It appears certain enough that the *Excelsis* fell there and that one or more explosions followed. Further than that, well, I frankly don't understand at present. There is more than the usual first report inaccuracy, but we ought to be able to clear it up before long.

'You gentlemen will have to appear before a magistrate, of course, but I think you may safely assume that there will be no difficulty about bail.'

He was quite right about that. There was a special and expeditious handling of our charge, and we were able to return to our families that evening. Sinderton went home, I know, with the same feeling as I did : that a day or two would see the whole mistaken business satisfactorily explained. But Captain Belford—well, perhaps he had a naturally more suspicious mind than we had, or it may have been some kind of premonition.

So far, the public had no interest in the affair. The reports were, of course, in all the evening papers, but even in those days nobody paid serious attention to an evening paper's headlines. So it can be said that the Belford affair, as it came to be known, really started the next day, with such introductions as :

'TREASURE SHIP WIPES OUT TOWN'

'GOLD ROCKET DESTROYS THOUSANDS'

'DEATH SHIP DROPS IN CITY'

The last was particularly effective on the contents bills; it left it to the readers to find out that the city referred to was not the City of London.

I bought several papers and read them carefully without learning much. They were all on much the same lines as yesterday's report. Pfaffheim was still taken to be a town of several thousands of working-class inhabitants, though a single explosion, not a series, was now reported. All reports still bore an appearance of being written up from meagre information. Nevertheless, in spite of its slender knowledge, *The Radiogram* seized the opportunity for improving the occasion with a leader in which it demanded a public inquiry and more than hinted at inefficiency and carelessness in the handling of salvage.

I read it through. It was in its usual vituperative style. I could not take it very seriously, and I did not suppose anyone else would. Who was going to believe that rather than open a few fuel-cocks we were going to run the risk of almost certainly losing our salvage money? Fuel is valuable, of course, but apart from anything else it must be obvious to everyone that the extra weight of full tanks would inevitably have torn the *Excelsis* free from her cables and crashed her.

I was still skimming the various accounts when the telephone rang and a voice told me that the D.A.C. of the Special Branch would be pleased to see me if I would step along about 12 o'clock. There are several ways of being invited to Scotland Yard. This one was perfectly amiable.

Captain Belford and Sinderton were already there when I was shown in. The D.A.C. and his secretary were the only others this time. The three were bending over a photograph on the desk. The D.A.C. pointed to it, and I looked more closely.

It showed a rocket-ship lying on her side. In the foreground and far into the background was a scene of desolation and utter destruction. Here and there were deep craters; the only vestiges of buildings were piles of bricks and rubble. The vista suggested a vast, dreary rubbish dump.

The angle at which the picture was taken showed that one side at least of the ship had been badly gashed and battered. Nevertheless, to those as well acquainted with her as we were, it was not difficult to recognise the old *Excelsis*.

While I was still looking at it, the Captain straightened up. 'What does this mean?' he asked the D.A.C.

The policeman took a cigarette and pushed across the box. 'As far as we can see it means quite a lot. I'm not sure how much yet, but I shall be surprised if it doesn't spell trouble of some kind.'

He offered us chairs.

'Perhaps the best aspect of it,' he went on, 'is that it will clear you gentlemen of the charge of negligence. It's perfectly obvious that if the *Excelsis* had been in fuel when she hit there wouldn't be a plate or a rivet of her to be found—but here she is, only a bit battered. No, it may be more serious than that.'

'Well, what did happen? Let's have it,' said the Captain.

The D.A.C. was not to be hurried.

'Since you were here we've been in touch with the Secret Service and learned quite a few interesting things. The chief one is that Pfaffheim ceased to be an agricultural village about two years ago. What you've done is to drop your *Excelsis* right into the centre of a new thriving and extremely hush-hush centre of explosives manufacture. As a result, you've achieved the destruction of five or six factories, wiped out an unknown number of storage depots, and utterly wrecked innumerable buildings. Furthermore, you have caused the sudden departure to Valhalla of several high officials, dozens of skilled chemists, to say nothing of between three and four thousand employees. That is what happened. And I may add that the authorities over there are very annoyed about it.'

He paused. 'They're even more annoyed that the report of the disaster got out. They moved fast, but not quite fast enough. It was too big a thing for even their censorship to hold in. News of a series of explosions was half across the world before they put out their official version of one explosion, and a British Agent had got this picture before they were reorganised enough to stop him.

'According to his report, the *Excelsis* landed right on top of one of the largest subterranean stores. He doesn't know the type of explosive stored there, but apparently it went off on concussion. Someone told him that so immense was the force of the explosion that the ship was blown into the air again and landed a full hundred yards to the side of its first hit. No one can say quite how that set off the rest, of course, but there seem to have been eight or ten major explosions, if not more.'

We were all a bit stunned. Our own satisfaction at being cleared from suspicion of neglect was rather damped down by the scale of the catastrophe.

'The Foreign Office,' the policeman went on, 'is inclined to link it up with reports that they've found a method of stabilising liquid oxygen bombs—which means very cheap production of explosives. They think that the stabilising may require several processes and the *Excelsis* concussed and set off some which were in an intermediate stage. The detonation of these might then conceivably have. . . .'

But we were in no mood for theoretical consideration of causes. Our own position was by now uppermost in our minds again. Captain Belford asked what all three of us wanted to know when he said :

'I suppose this means that the charge against us will be dropped?'

The other broke off and switched his attention to this side of the affair.

'You will have to attend the hearing, I'm afraid. But it will only be a matter of a few minutes. The police will inform the magistrate that in the light of further information they do not wish to proceed. That will dispose of the police side. The formal Government inquiry into the loss of the *Excelsis* is a different matter; that will take place in the usual course.'

It was a relief to all of us to hear that. It is a funny thing that for most men the whitest conscience is no protection from some apprehension in the presence of the police.

CHAPTER SIX

CRIMINALS OF SPACE

WE three had lunch together and went our ways with the feeling that it had all blown over quite satisfactorily for us. The prospect of a formal inquiry did not worry us: after all, that follows in three out of every four cases of salvage. For me the feeling lasted until 7 o'clock when I read in a late evening edition that Captain William Belford had been arrested at his house at Highgate.

I found the news in the stop-press after I had read the rest of the paper. They had, it appeared, now discovered that Pfaffheim was not an agricultural village, but they cautiously refrained from saying just what it was. However, I noticed that some emphasis was laid on the series of explosions in contrast to the official report. I only happened to notice the sentence in the stop-press by accident; two minutes later I was on the 'phone to Scotland Yard. I gave my name and they put me through to the D.A.C. at once.

'What's this about arresting the Captain?' I demanded. 'Have they repeated yesterday's news or something?'

'No. It's right enough,' he told me. 'We've been looking for you, too. Where are you?'

'What's it about?' I asked cautiously.

'It's about murder and attempted murder. You didn't go home this afternoon did you?'

'No. I'm just on my way there now.'

'Well, change your mind. I want you round here as soon as you can manage it.'

'But. . . .'

'No buts. This is serious. I'll tell you when you come.'

I hesitated.

'All right. In about ten minutes,' I told him.

'Glad you saw that news,' he said, as I entered. 'We hoped you would. Didn't know how else to get at you before you went home.'

'But you said this morning....' I began.

'Oh, this morning. That's different. Let me tell you this. If you'd gone home you'd most likely not be alive now. Captain Belford was shot at and wounded in front of his house about half-past three. Mr. Sinderton was murdered on his own doorstep about the same time. It's ten to one they were ready for you, too.'

'Sinderton dead?' I said, incredulously.

'With five bullets. The Captain had only a flesh wound in the arm, luckily.'

I just gaped at him.

'But I don't understand. Who...? What...? What do you mean, ready for me?'

'I mean that your two friends were the subjects of deliberate attacks—And I'm pretty sure you would have been, too, if they'd known where to find you.'

'But I don't understand,' I said again. 'Who do you mean by "they?" Who on earth would want to shoot me?'

'Might it not be some friends or—er—associates of the people at Pfaffheim?' he suggested.

I pulled myself together and considered. I couldn't see it.

'Quite unlikely, I should say,' I returned, pretty calmly. 'What on earth would be the good of that? What would be the point of shooting us on account of an accident? It's not sensible.'

'I don't know,' he said slowly. 'But can you think of any other reason why there should be attempts on them both?'

'I can't think of any reason at all. What you suggest certainly isn't a reason,' I told him.

'Possibly you're right. We shall see. At any rate, I shall be glad if you will make arrangements to stay away from home for a night or two until it is cleared up.'

I argued with him a bit. I couldn't see any reason why I was in danger, but he was persuasive. Without actually putting it into words, he somehow suggested that there was a lot at the back of the business. By the time he got through I had an uneasy feeling that any corner might hide a gunman waiting for me. It's not a nice sensation. In the end I agreed to stay, though not without a sense that I was scared of a shadow.

Either the Secret Service had released their photograph or some enterprising journalist had contrived to smuggle out another, for there was the picture of the damaged *Excelsis*, among the debris she was supposed to have caused, large in every paper, and on the front page of most. It made it clear to everyone that the ship had not blown up. Furthermore, the later editions ran a translation from German papers. Realising that their censorship had broken down, they were shouting their heads off with another theory.

The whole thing, we learned, was an infamous plot. Jewish influence, combining behind the Jewish Captain Belford, had aimed a blow at the defences of the Reich; the first blow in the covert war which World Jewry was opening against Germany: the blood of two thousand five hundred German martyrs was on their heads. Investigations by the Gestapo had revealed that Captain Belford and his officers had been bribed to the extent of £250,000 to drop the *Excelsis* on the defenceless town of Pfaffheim and to make it appear an accident. It was no accident. It was a bolt fired at Germany and German defence. The two thousand five hundred Aryan Germans who had been its victims had fallen for the Fatherland as truly as any soldier in the field. They would be avenged. The people of the Third Reich demanded that the murderers be surrendered to German justice.

The well-known technique of 'the big lie' was at work again. I had been given quarters with the Captain and we read the stuff through together, marvelling that anyone should find it worth printing.

'But I'm not a Jew,' said the Captain, bewilderedly.

'What do you think that matters?' I said. 'You're accused of an anti-Nazi plot, so you must be a Jew.'

'And how the hell do they think I did it? Don't they know that even under the best conditions you can't be sure within fifty miles either side where a derelict will fall?'

'Of course they know. But does the public? After all don't we spend a deuce of a lot of time trying to convince them of the accuracy and dependability of the Rocket Service?'

'Two-fifty thousand. H'm. It'd almost have been worth trying,' muttered the Captain.

The D.A.C., accompanied by the Assistant Commissioner himself, came to visit us.

'Well,' he said, as his eye fell on the papers. 'They're out for your blood, aren't they? We've already had a demand from the Embassy for your extradition.'

'I'll sue them for libel,' said the Captain.

'In a German court?' asked the Assistant Commissioner, with a smile.

'But this stuff's all rot. They must know that,' I protested.

'Of course they do. But they're out to get you one way or another, aren't they?' he pointed to the sling which held the

Captain's arm. 'The question is why?'

'It's absurd. A state doesn't revenge itself like that on individuals for what it knows must have been a pure accident,' I told him.

'Quite. I agree. So there must be another reason, mustn't there?'

'But what?'

'Have you forgotten the *Excelsis*'s cargo? There was gold, they're very short of that.'

The Captain gave a snort. He showed signs of launching himself on one of his customary attacks on gold, but thought better of it.

'And there was ganywood—nearly as valuable. And there was a lot of tillfer fibre—how about that?'

It was an aspect which had not struck me before. Tillfer fibre under treatment produces Etherium, the lightest known gas; we used to use it in the wings of 'planes to give added lift, among other things. Since tillfer grows only on Ganymede and in limited quantities there, and also because there was an Anglo-American trade protectorate in force there, the Germans couldn't get it. It was one of the raw materials they felt sore about. Hard on them, of course, but how much would they have let us have if it had been their trade protectorate? That's an easy answer.

'So what?' I asked.

'I don't know. But suppose, just suppose, they would only hand over that cargo on condition you were turned over to them.'

'Would that do them any good?'

'They could claim for their own people's benefit to have dealt with plotters as they should be dealt with.'

'Fantastic. Who's going to believe that?' the Captain asked.

The Assistant Commissioner shrugged his shoulders.

'Quite a lot of people if it's shouted loudly enough. The same kind of thing has worked often before. It's wonderful what they take.' He ruminated a few moments. 'They made a mess of 1914. They came a cropper in 1940. And now they're working up for it again. You know, when I look at them, I know just how Henry the Second must have seen Thomas à Becket.'

But the A.C. was wrong. Public indignation over the demand worked up quickly, and, as ever, concentrated in groups on various aspects: against the presumptuous belief that the handing over of British subjects to a foreign court could be tolerated for a moment: against the existence of any plot:

against the feasibility of such an arrangement. The calmest partisans suggested that there should be a trial for the purpose of clearing us, but that it should be held in England where a sense of justice and not the good of the state could be relied on to produce a verdict.

The next day the situation was inflamed. Reports of the murder of Sinderton and the attempt on Captain Belford were published. We learned that the Embassy was still pressing for our extradition on the ground that we had, in dropping the derelict from no charted territory, committed an act of piracy which placed us beyond the protection of our government.

A news message from Germany went one better. The *Excelsis*, it said, carried no cargo. She was an empty hulk. This, they claimed, was substantiated by a member of the crew who had confessed that we had stopped at the Moon and hidden the cargo there before coming on to Earth.

The Captain and I gasped over this latest piece of effrontery. They had gone one better than the A.C.'s prophecy: they wanted both us and the cargo.

Well, maybe their own people believed that about the cargo, but it didn't go down too well over here at first. It takes civilised people quite a while to appreciate 'the big lie' technique.

It was queer, too, why we should bother to drop an empty hulk when it might have been full of explosives as they had previously claimed. But they didn't seem to bother about little points like that. It was years later that some journalist dug up the story of the treasure on the Moon and people began wondering about it.

At the time, the whole thing seemed to us to be just farcical. However, when the Assistant Commissioner came to see us once more it turned out to be not so humorous after all.

'They want you over there,' he said. 'You realise what that means. Execution. And more. Before you are condemned they'll have a confession out of you by some means that you stole the *Excelsis*'s cargo and hid it on the Moon. They'll brand you as both pirates and criminals.

'We, naturally, have no wish to surrender you. But, and it is a big but, according to international law their claim is perfectly good. A person accused of engineering a crime in free space is eligible for trial in the country of the plaintiff.'

That was a facer. Naturally, until that moment, we had neither of us given serious consideration to the German claim.

'It puts us in an awkward position,' he went on, for all the world as if it didn't put us in a jam. 'It boils down to this.

Either we must hand you over and connive at what we know to be injustice, or else we must commit a flagrant breach of international law.

'We have, I repeat, no wish to do the former. Yet, in our position can we do the latter?

'The Government is very worried over you two. You see, you have a political aspect, too, now. Foreign relations are none too easy; it's no time to flout international agreements. On the other hand, the party majority at home is none too stable. Any big popular outcry will almost certainly result in their losing the next election: and handing you over would raise an almighty shindy.'

I felt that if we were to be political counters it was extremely lucky that we had the feeling of the people with us.

'As I, and several who are much more influential than I, see it,' he went on, 'there is one remedy, and one only. You two are going to have to disappear.'

'Disappear?'

'Make an escape—preferably a spectacular escape—from custody.'

'I don't like that,' said the Captain. 'I'm a man with a clean record. I've done nothing I'm ashamed of. I ought to have a chance to clear myself.'

'Of course, you don't like it. Nor do we. But you'd like still less being made to sign a false confession.'

'Let them try to make me.'

'I'd rather not,' said the Assistant Commissioner. There was a lot of unpleasant suggestion in his voice. It took quite a time to din a full realisation of the position into the Captain, he was so satisfied with the clearness of his own innocence. It was an hour before we could get him to see the thing in the round, so to speak.

Then there was a lot to arrange. False names, and passports. A method by which his wife could also disappear and join him. Money to be banked for us under our new names. But we got it all fixed at last, with the Captain still looking a bit bewildered as if his sense of values had been turned upside down.

Well, that's about where truth ends and legend begins, and as everyone knows the legends, I need not repeat them here.

It seems a pity in a way to spoil a daring and exciting exploit this way, but, as you see, with the whole thing beautifully stage-managed and all guns loaded with blanks it wasn't really too difficult. We just shot off into the blue.

I kept my new name for some years until the whole thing had blown over and when I changed it back no one thought of identifying me with the escaped Fearon. Belford's name had become too well known, so he had to stick to his new one for the rest of his life.

My hope is that this account will at last put a stop to these perpetual treasure hunts to the Moon. Several lives and a lot of money have been thrown away on them. Once and for all, then; Captain Belford's treasure does not exist. It never did.

CHILD OF POWER

CHAPTER ONE

OF MICE AND MEN

IT was one of those evenings more often imagined than
granted in the Lake District. The stir in the air scarcely
ruffled the water and it was warm enough to enjoy sitting out
on the terrace after sunset. Peace had crept gradually over the
valley to settle down finally with the closing of the public bar.
The peak of the mountain opposite was still silhouetted
against the lingering afterglow, lights occasionally wandered
across its black base and the sound of a car engine came over
the lake to us no louder than the buzz of a bumble bee. One
sat and drank beer and smoked and chatted.

We were a chance-met group, such as any pub in the district
might have held that night. A business man and his son from
somewhere in Lancashire, two American college boys energeti-
cally seeing England from bicycles bought within an hour of
their arrival at Southampton, a tall man in whose speech was a
faint suggestion of the north Midlands, his wife, and Joan and
myself. The four others in the place, two young men and
young women whose notion of a holiday seemed to consist of
dissipating the maximum of ergs in the minimum of time, had
already left us in order that no mountain might put them to
shame on the morrow.

Conversationally, we had rambled quite a way. We had considered the inhabitants and character of the neighbourhood,
thence we had somehow arrived at the Spanish question and
settled that, which had entailed our decision that certain social
reforms were vitally necessary all over the world, and this in
its turn had led us to speculation on the future in general and
the future of man in particular. One of the Americans was
touched into eloquence on the subject.

'It's such a darned muddle in most people's minds,' he said.
'They know that nothing is really static, it's all got to change,
but along with that they're convinced that modern man is
God's last word—and yet that's contradicted again because if
they were as convinced of it as they think they are they'd do
something to straighten out the system and make it a decent

world for this climax of evolution to live in—to settle down in permanently.'

'As it is,' put in his companion, 'they just tinker away at it a bit because instinct rather than reason tells them that it's a waste of time to make the perfect social set-up for our kind of man when he may be superseded by another kind who won't be satisfied with that set-up at all.'

'What do you mean by another kind of man?' asked the Lancashire man from behind his pipe. 'What other kind can there be?'

'What about a type with a super brain?' suggested his son. 'Something like "The Hampdenshire Wonder" that Beresford wrote about, or Stapledon's "Odd John." Didn't you read those books?'

'No, I didn't,' his father said, bluntly. 'I've something better to do with my time than readin' tales about fancies and freaks.'

'It's only the form,' said his son. 'What they're suggesting is that the next step will be a great brain development.'

'Oh, aye. Chaps wi' big 'eads, and suchlike. I don't believe it.'

'That's not the only possibility,' put in Joan, beside me. 'I think the next step will be psychic. Perhaps telepathy, or a kind of clairvoyance that can really be used; or perhaps they'll be able to see things that we can't see now—as some people say animals can.'

'Sounds retrogressive to me,' the first American told her. 'I'd say most of those things did exist in man, and do in animals to a certain extent now, but that they've atrophied with the development of the brain. No, I guess brain development's the way it goes. Though in a way I'd say you're right about seeing things. Eyes are still improving. Maybe they'll be able to see the infra-red or the ultra-violet, and p'raps some emanations we know nothing about. But I think the brain and the reasoning faculties will gradually develop beyond anything we can conceive at present.'

'Why gradually?' asked his friend. 'There doesn't seem to have been much change in the last five thousand years. Why not at a jump?—that's the way with mutations.'

'Maybe, but how do you think a sudden mutation is going to survive boneheads like us? We'd probably put it out of the way out of kindness, or lock it up in an asylum and not let it breed. I can see us defending ourselves mighty toughly against any mutations.'

'And very right, too,' said the Lancashire man. ''Oo wants to breed freaks or mutilations or whatever they are? Put 'em out of their misery, be 'umane, I say.'

'But they wouldn't be freaks, Father. If they were the natural next step in development, they'd be normal.'

'If they 'ad big 'eads and thought different from other people they'd be freaks. A big 'ead's a freak, same as a bearded woman. I've seen 'em at Blackpool. A man's the same as the rest of us or 'e's a freak. Stands to reason.'

The tall man from the Midlands spoke out of the darkness to the Americans.

'I think you're right about the jump, but what sort of a jump's it going to be? That's the question. It can't be too big a physical change at one step. We, just like the wild animals, hate a variation from our norm, and I agree we'd be pretty sure to suppress it for a humane or for any other reason which happened to suit us. No, we must have survived to reach this stage by taking a series of small and not very obvious jumps in safety.'

'But small jumps would mean pretty frequent jumps, or we'd never have had time to get from the amoeba to here.' said one of the Americans. 'Now, if there's been a jump worth a nickel in the last five thousand years I've not heard of it. That's surely a long time to stay put. Maybe we have come to the end or maybe nobody's noticed it when it happened.'

'Or,' said the tall man, 'maybe it's just about to happen.' He puffed at his cigarette so that it glowed and lit up his face. One had a feeling from his tone that he was not just speaking at random. The American asked:

'You've an idea what it might be?'

'*Might* be—well, yes. But, mind you, I'm laying no claim to prophecy. As far as I go is to say that I have seen a variation from the normal which does not seem to be due to any of those glandular upsets which commonly cause freaks. It is, to the best of my knowledge, unique, but, of course, there may be others. If there are, I see no reason why they should not survive and stabilise the new type.'

'Which is?' prompted the American.

'An additional sense. A sixth sense.' There was a slightly disappointed pause.

'Well, I don't know that there's much in that,' said the Lancashire man. 'Means knowing things as nobody told you, and you 'aven't read. There's a word for it—oh, aye, intuition, that's it. Young lady I once knew 'ad it. She went into the fortune reading business. Didn't do so bad, either.'

'That's not what I mean,' the tall man told him a trifle shortly. 'I'm not talking about a mixture of guesswork, humbug and adding two and two. I mean a real sense. with organs of perception as real as your eyes and your ears and your nose and your tongue.'

'I don't see as you need any more. They're enough, aren't they?'

The rest ignored him.

'Organs for the perception of what?' asked the elder American curiously.

The tall man did not reply at once. He turned up the end of his cigarette and regarded it for a moment.

'All right,' he said. 'I'll tell you about it. But I warn you that all the names and places will be faked. If there is any chance of following the business up, I want to do it myself.'

CHAPTER TWO

THE STRANGE CASE OF TED FILLER

THE tall man paused again as though seeking an opening.

'It's an odd little story, and to explain to you how I come to know so much about it, I shall have to reveal that I practise medicine. That's a thing I keep quiet as a rule when I am away from home. It alters people's attitude if they know it and shuts one off from them almost as much as if one were a clergyman.

'However, that is my profession and for twenty years, until, in fact, two years ago when I moved south, I practised in Irkwell in Derbyshire. It's a place which is typical of the kind of semi-industrialised village you find round there. Most of the men are employed in the quarries or the mills, a few work lead in the pits where there's any left to work. The women work in the mills, too, until they marry and start having more children than they want. The place is partly cottages of local stone but mostly rows of shoddy cottages put up in the last century when the mills came. In general, it's a kind of semi-rural slum. Not the kind of place you'd expect to produce any advance on modern humanity—and yet there's no doubt in my mind that young Ted Filler was something more than an ordinary freak.

'His mother, Ada, regarded his arrival more as an act of God than a personal achievement until she found out that he was a boy. It was a discovery which had the result of infusing more interest into the family life. Her three previous contributions had all been girls, and this, and the deaths of the two younger in infancy, had helped to give her an attitude of discouraged fatalism about the whole business. But with Ted's birth she seemed to make a fresh start and he began his independent existence enviably protected by first child devotion and fourth child experience.

'Not that he appeared to be in the least in need of special treatment. He was a healthy, well-formed child whose yells when he was washed were encouragingly lusty. I did not detect the least sign of abnormality in him, nor do I think would anyone else have done so. I was able with complete honesty to assure his father and mother that they had a remarkably fine son—and that wasn't too common in my Irkwell practice.

'Nevertheless, when I called on Mrs. Filler again I found satisfaction somewhat diluted.

' " 'E worries us, 'e does," she said. "Not but what 'e ain't a dear little chap and me proud of 'im," she added, in the manner of one anxious not to appear ungrateful. "But 'e ain't like the others was. 'E's that difficult to get to sleep, you'd never believe. And then sometimes when you've got 'im to sleep 'e'll wake up all of a sudden and look at you just like 'e's 'ad the fright of 'is little life, then 'e'll begin to 'owl. Ee, an' 'e does 'owl. Fair frightened me and Jim first time 'e done it. We thought 'e wasn't never going to stop. An 'e didn't, not till 'e was fair wore out—and so was we. I'd like you to 'ave a look at 'im, Doctor, if you will. I don't feel easy about him, an' that's a fact."

'I gave the child a careful examination. From what I knew of Ada Filler I was fairly certain she wasn't one to get worked up unnecessarily, though of course you can never be sure. The baby was lying in its cot, blue eyes wide open, but quite quiet and peaceful. There didn't seem to be a thing as it shouldn't be and I said so.

' "I'm glad to 'ear that," said his mother. "Still—I don't know. 'E'll lie quiet that way for hours when you'd think 'e'd be asleep, then all of a sudden, for no reason, off 'e'll go like a 'ooter. An' nowt as I can do'll stop 'im."

'Well, there wasn't anything really to worry about. Some children are like that; they take one look at the world and hate it on sight and you can't blame them much in a place like Irkwell, but in the end they learn to put up with it, like the rest of us. Nevertheless, young Ted Filler seemed to be taking his time about settling down. Whenever I looked in during the next few weeks it was the same tale. Once or twice I heard him howling. It was a remarkable achievement. I didn't wonder that his parents were looking worn and that the rest of the street was behaving pretty offensively to them.

' " 'E don't sleep enough, not near enough," his father assured me. " 'T'ain't natural. 'T'ain't fair on a man as 'as to work, either." '

All I could tell them was that I'd stake my reputation there was nothing wrong with the child and that he would soon outgrow it.

'It was two months later that something occurred which might have given me an early clue to the whole thing had I had the wit to perceive it as a clue.

'I had called at the Fillers' cottage about something to do with their daughter, Doreen, I think, and naturally inquired after the baby.

' "Oh, I found out what to do with 'im," his mother said.

'She showed me. The heir of the Fillers was sleeping peacefully and with an expression of blissful satisfaction. His bed was made up in an ordinary galvanised iron bath with a handle each end. He could have passed for an Italian cherub or a patent food advertisement.

' "Sleeps pretty near all the time now. Makin' up for it, like," she said.

' "How did you do it?" I asked.

'She explained that it had happened by accident a week or two before. She had been ironing when Ted started one of his howls. She had fetched him down to the kitchen because, even if you couldn't stop him, you could keep an eye on him, but no sooner had she got him downstairs than the insurance man had called.

'The baby had to be put somewhere while she got the money and paid the man and the handiest place for the moment was on top of the clean linen stacked in one of the tin baths. When she came back from the door he had not only stopped crying but was fast asleep, so she left him there as long as possible. The next time he yelled she did the same again, and with the same result. It seemed to work every time.

' "So now I makes 'is bed in there regular," she added. "Seems queer, but it suits 'im. Good as gold, 'e is, in there. Won't sleep nowhere else."

'I didn't take much notice at the time. A preference for sleeping in a tin bath just seemed one of those odd infantile idiosyncrasies which the wise accept and use gratefully.

'Well, time went on. I used to look in at the Fillers'

occasionally, so I saw young Ted from time to time. I didn't take a great interest in him for he was a healthy enough baby. I gathered that he persisted in his odd preference for sleeping in a tin bath, but beyond that he seemed undistinguished. And yet, when I came to think it over afterwards, there was another incident which might have given me a hint.

'On that occasion he was lying in a dilapidated perambulator outside the back door. He did not show that he noticed me. His eyes were wide open, gazing far away, but he was not quite silent; he seemed to be humming a little tune. As I bent over him I could swear I caught that theme from the New World Symphony. You know how it goes.'

The doctor broke off and hummed a few bars.

'That was what it seemed. Hummed by a child one year old. I was curious enough to ask Mrs. Filler whether she had heard it on the wireless and learned that the family taste fancied variety, sports news and cinema organs almost exclusively. I remember thinking that even if the child had happened to hear a version on a cinema organ he showed astonishing tonal memory, and then for one reason or another I forgot the incident until later. Probably, I very reasonably told myself that I had made just a foolish mistake.

'I must have seen the child several times during the next two or three years, but I admit I've no recollection of doing so, for, as I said, he was too healthy to be really interesting, though I wish now I'd kept an eye on him. It was not until his boy was over four that Jim Filler came to see me one Monday evening and gave me an interest in the boy which I'm never likely to lose.

'Jim had cleaned up and polished off the quarry dust for the occasion. He seemed a bit uncertain of himself.

' "I don't want to waste your time, Doctor," he said, "but I would be grateful if you'd come, casual-like, and 'ave a look at our Ted sometime when me and the missus is there."

' "What's wrong with him?" I said.

'Jim fiddled his cap in his hands.

' "I don't know as there's owt wrong with 'im, exactly," he said. "It's—it's, well, 'e's a bit queer, some'ow, in a manner o' speakin'. It's got me and the missus fair worried an' all. She don't know as I've come 'ere. So if you could drop in kind of accidental like, you know——?"

' "But what's wrong with him?" I asked again. "Do you think he's backward; not up to the rest, or something like that?"

' "Nay, t'lad's bright enough that way. 'Taint nothin' o'

that kind. Fact, some ways 'e's a bit too bright, that's a funny thing. 'E don't often talk like a nipper and many's the time I've 'eard 'im use words what I'm sure 'e ain't never 'eard from me and the missus. Understands what's said to 'im, too, better than any kid I know."

'I asked a few more questions, but Jim seemed to be holding back for some reason or other. If it had been another man I might have been short with him, but I knew Jim. His type is the incarnation of stubborn commonsense. In the end I got rid of him by promising to go round the next evening, though I didn't expect to find much amiss.'

CHAPTER THREE

THE BOY WHO SAW SOUND

'EVIDENTLY Jim Filler had changed his mind and told his wife that I was coming, for she didn't seem surprised to see me. In honour of the occasion they took me into the front room, an apartment with a curious stage-set appearance, but I stopped Ada Filler as she was putting a match to the fire and suggested that we all went to the kitchen. We'd all feel more natural and less Sunday-best in there, as well as warmer.

'Even so, it wasn't easy to begin. Neither of them was anxious to come out plainly with the trouble. We had to exchange a number of ineffective sentences before Jim cut through it and became his usual forthright self again. He put on a dogged expression.

' "I know it'll sound daft, Doctor, but it's God's truth. Me and the missus's ready to swear to that, so if you'll 'ear me right through——?"

' "Go ahead and tell me. I'll ask questions afterwards," I assured him.

' "Well, this is 'ow it was. Saturday tea time we was all in 'ere waitin' for news on t'wireless so as I could check my coupons——" he began.

'It certainly was an odd tale that Jim had to tell.

'Mrs. Filler had been setting the table, while her husband and the two children waited for their tea. Jim had copies of his pool entries and a pencil ready to check them. At six o'clock he switched on to Droitwich. It meant that they'd have to listen to the weather forecast and a lot of political talk before

the important stuff came along, but you could never be sure
how long it would take to get the sports bulletin and it wasn't
worth risking missing any of it. Well, he switched on all right
and the dial lit up, but nothing came out of the speaker. He
pressed the switch on and off a bit and looked at the outside
connections. They were right enough.

' "Eeh-h-h, there's summat wrong wi' t' bastard, there is, an'
all," he decided.

'He turned the set round and took off the back. It looked all
right, at least there was nothing obviously adrift. He scratched
his head. It's not as easy to trace trouble in a modern mains set
as it was in the old battery days. The insides look alarmingly
efficient.

'It was then that young Ted took an interest.

' "What's oop with it, Dad?" he asked, coming closer.

' " 'Ow should I know?" inquired Jim, with irritation.

'Well, it was then that the strange thing happened. Jim said
that young Ted had looked at him "sort of surprised like,"
then the child had pushed in between him and the set. He
didn't look inside it, Jim said; he put his head down at it as if
he were going to butt it, then he lifted his face again and
looked at his father.

' "It's in there. That's where it stops," he said and pointed to
a black object in the cabinet.

' "It were a transformer," Jim said. "An' 'e were right, too.
Chap 'ad a look at it yesterday and one of the windin's was
gone."

'Later, Jim had remembered another "funny thing."

'Several weeks previously he had been taking his son for a
Sunday walk. They were on the Derby road where the grid
lines run almost alongside when young Ted looked up at a
pylon for no reason and said suddenly, "It's stopped."

'Jim couldn't make out what he was talking about and
probably didn't care much, but he remembered that on the
way back young Ted, equally without reason, had said, "It's
going again, now."

'It wasn't until he got back that he learned there had been a
breakdown somewhere which had put the grid out of action
for half an hour or so.

'But he only recalled that afterwards. At the moment, he
was chiefly concerned over the prospect of missing his football
news.

' Now I'll 'ave to go and buy t'Football Special, when
t'papers come in," he groused.

'Young Ted had made no immediate reply to that. He had sat silent for a while looking rather puzzled, then with the air of one who had considered the subject unsatisfactorily from all angles he said:

' "Why, Dad?"

' "Why, what?" asked Jim, whose mind had gone on.

' "Why'll you 'ave to get a paper?"

' "Because," explained Jim, patiently, "because we can't 'ave t'bloody wireless, that's why."

'There was a pause while young Ted took this in.

' 'D'you mean you can't 'ear what the man's sayin'?" he inquired.

' "Course that's what I mean. 'Ow d'you think any of us is goin' to 'ear owt now t'set's busted? You shut up, and eat your tea."

'There was another pause.

' "I can," said young Ted thoughtfully.

' "You can what?"

' " 'Ear what 'e's sayin'."

'Jim transferred his gaze from his tripe to his son. He looked at him hard for some moments without speaking. He didn't want to turn on the lad for lying if it was only some childish make-believe game.

' "Well, tell us what t'chap is sayin', then," he invited.

'Young Ted did. "Brentford, one," he said. "Stoke City, nought. Derby County, nought. Birmingham, one. Everton, two. . . ."

' "An' 'e were right," Jim went on, leaning forward. "I know 'e were right. I checked 'em up on my list as 'e said 'em, an' then I went out an' got t'paper to make sure. 'E were dead right, every time."

'Ada Filler went on as he stopped.

' "I never 'eard of nothin' like it. It don't seem natural. Do you think it's dangerous, Doctor?"

'I looked at them, feeling pretty puzzled. There was no doubt they believed what they said. Jim was in dead earnest and a bit worried. Ada was more worried; she showed all that maternal solicitude which so oddly hopes that its child will be outstanding while being absolutely normal, distinguished while being indistinguishable.

'I was at a loss for a reply. In my mind I was searching for a set of circumstances which could possibly produce the appearance of what they believed to have happened, and I could not find one at the moment. There floated into my mind the memory of the child's curious humming as it lay in its perambulator, over three years ago now. Curiosity prompted me to ask.

' "Is Ted fond of music?"

' "Well, 'e can't play anything," Mrs. Filler said, "It's early days for that, ain't it? But 'e's often 'ummin' things, all sorts of tunes I never 'eard of."

'Jim was looking at me.

' "You don't believe it, Doctor? Not that 'e was really 'earin' the wireless without a set, I mean?"

' "Well, it takes a bit of swallowing you know, Jim. Would you believe it if you were in my position? There must be some explanation."

' "Oh, there's that, all right, but it'll be a queer one, not a trick one. I'll get t'lad down 'ere and you'll see."

'He left the room. We heard him clatter upstairs and then down again. He came in carrying young Ted in his arms and put him down in a chair. The little boy sat there, sleepy and perhaps a trifle pale, though he looked well enough otherwise.

' "Now, Ted, lad, tell t'doctor what's on t'National now."

' "Ain't it mended?" said Ted, eyeing the wireless set on the dresser.

' "Aye, it's all right. But you just tell 'im what's on t'National."

'Young Ted appeared to think for a moment, then:

' "Music," he said. "Loud music."

' " 'Ow does it go?" his father persisted.

'Ted began to hum a part of a march quite recognisably one of Sousa's, I think.

' "That's right, lad. Now you keep on 'ummin'," said Jim, and switched on the radio set.

'Nobody spoke while the set warmed up. The only sound was Ted humming his march with a fine martial air. Jim leaned over and turned the volume control. A march came flooding out of the speaker. It was the same tune exactly on the beat and in pitch with Ted's humming.

'I couldn't think of anything to say. I just sat staring at the child. Jim turned the volume control right down to nothing and reset the dial.

' "What's on Regional?" he asked his son.

' "People clappin'," said young Ted with the briefest pause. "Now there's two men talking."

' "Sayin' what?"

' "Good evening, cads," said young Ted, in a travestied drawl.

'Jim turned the knob. The weary-toned wit of the Western Brothers pervaded the room.

' "What else?" Jim asked, damping out again.

' "Lots of things. A man shouting very loud over there." Ted pointed to a corner of the room. He lapsed into a gabble which sounded like a vocal cartoon of German.

' "Try Berlin," I suggested to Jim.

' "That's 'im," said young Ted, between the bolts of impassioned rhetoric which leapt out at us.

'Jim gave it a few moments and then switched off.

' "Well, there it is, Doctor," he said.

'There, indeed, it was, unmistakably. And I was supposed to make something of it.

'I looked at the boy. He was not paying attention to us. There was an abstracted expression on his face, not vacant in the least, but preoccupied. As his father said:

' " 'Tain't no wonder 'e seems dreamy-like sometimes if 'e's got that goin' on in 'is head all the while."

' "Ted," I asked him, "do you hear that all the time?"

'He came out of his abstraction and looked at me.

' "Aye," he said, "when it's going."

'It occurred to me then for the first time that I had been thinking of him—and that he had behaved—as if he were quite twice his age or more.

' "Does it worry you?"

' "No," he said, a bit uncertainly, " 'cept at night, and when it's so loud I 'ave to look at it."

'He always used that queer hybrid of expression. He talked about "quiet" and "loud" and yet coupled them with "looking."

' "At night?" I asked.

' "Aye, it's loud then."

' "Always puts a tin box over 'is 'ead at nights, 'e does," his mother put in. "I've tried to stop 'im time and again. Doesn't seem natural, not to sleep with yer 'ead in a tin box, it doesn't. But 'e would 'ave it, and it does keep 'im quiet. 'Course, I didn't know about this 'ere. 'E just said it were noises and music, and I thought it were fancies."

'I remembered the tin bath of his babyhood.

' "Does the box stop it?" I asked him.

' "Middlin'," said young Ted.

' "Maybe," I said cautiously, 'we could stop it altogether at nights somehow. Would you like that?"

' "Aye."

' "Well, come here and let me have a look at you."

'His mother stretched out her hand and brought him over under the light.

'As I've told you there was nothing at all unusual about his appearance, it was just that of any normal little boy. With the story of the tin and the memory of Jim's description of him as he bent at the wireless set, I put my hands on his head and began to feel the structure. It wasn't long before I came on something decidedly unusual.

'On either side of the vault of the skull, about two inches above the temples, I found a round, soft spot about the size of a halfpenny. Hair grew on the spots as thickly as on the rest of the skull, but there was certainly no bone beneath, and the spots were situated with exact symmetry. The child winced involuntarily as my fingers touched them.

' "Does that hurt?" I asked him.

'His "no" sounded a little doubtful.

'I told him to close his eyes and then touched the lids with the tips of my fingers. It brought exactly the same wincing reaction. I was aware of a curiously excited feeling growing inside me. I had never heard of anything at all like this. It was unique. I parted the hair over the soft spots and looked closely. The skin was continuous and unbroken. There was nothing to see. Again I cautiously explored the spots with my fingers. The child did not like it. He dodged and broke away from me.

'I was aware of his parents looking at me expectantly, but I kept my eyes on young Ted. I was trying to control my own excitement. I think an astronomer who has found a new planet or an explorer who has discovered a new continent must have felt rather as I felt then. Unable to believe his own luck and busily cramming his imagination down with reason; seeking for a hold on the hard facts and their implications.

'I had an automatic desire to keep the child as unaware as possible of his singularity and an instinctive impulse to belittle its importance for his parents' benefit. The motives for that impulse were, I confess, mixed. In fact, I've never really been able to sort them out honestly yet. There was a professional desire not to be sensational, undoubtedly a jealous wish to keep the thing to myself for the time being until I could learn more about it, and probably a lot of others.

'His mother took the child upstairs again and I waited for her to come back before I said anything, then I was deliberately matter of fact.

' "It's unusual, most unusual," I told them, "but it's certainly not anything to be frightened about. It's an extra sensitivity which, I confess, I don't altogether understand at present, but we shall undoubtedly learn more about that from talking to him and watching him, now that we know what to look for. I'd like you to observe very closely all he does or says with reference to electricity and let me know in as much detail as you can. His general health appears to be perfectly good, but if you like I'll go over him thoroughly tomorrow.

'"One thing strikes me, and that is that perhaps he's not getting enough sleep, or not sleeping soundly when he does. We may be able to get over that by giving him a better shield than a tin box. About the rest of it, his being so forward for his age in the way he speaks and understands questions, and that kind of thing—I don't think you need worry either. It's rather soon to be definite about anything yet, but it does seem likely that if he has had this kind of thing going on all the time the constant stimulation may have forced his brain to develop abnormally fast. He doesn't laugh much, does he?"

'"No, 'e's a solemn one."

'"Well, you know, I'd say at a guess that his brain's pretty tired. You see, it gets no rest from this, night or day, except perhaps when he's sleeping—we can't tell that for certain until we know more about it—and that's bound to tire him. Besides, although it must stimulate in one way, yet in another it deadens because it gives his mind no chance to develop along its own lines. We shall have to find a way of altering that. It may not be very difficult.

'"I'm very glad you called me in now because, though of course we don't know how he actually feels it, it's difficult to believe that it isn't putting a considerable strain on him, and the sooner we can relieve the strain to some extent, the easier he will find things.

'"There's nothing to worry about. I'll come round tomorrow, as I said, and perhaps I shall be able to explain more about it"

'I left them puzzled, though considerably, if vaguely, reassured. But I myself went home with my mind revolving unrestrainedly around the most astounding discovery. The boy had a sixth sense, something I had never heard, read or dreamed of. But from that moment I had not a vestige of doubt that young Ted was—the word seemed to coin itself—electro-sentient.'

CHAPTER FOUR

STRANGE NEW WORLD

THE tall man paused. His face became suddenly visible in the darkness as he lit another cigarette.

'It must be difficult for a non-medical man to appreciate all that meant to me,' he went on. 'There were so many sides to it. The sheerly professional interest, the fact oneself and no other had the opportunity to study it, the evolutionary aspect and the question of whether such a thing would become stabilised, the developments which would ensue if it did, as well as the work to be done in determining its capacities, limitations and nature.

'Some people would say, I've no doubt, that I should, in the interests of science, have announced the discovery—and so I shall one day—but you can judge the playing up and sensationalism which would have swamped us and made quiet, normal observation impossible. Imagine what would happen when the newspapers got it—it would be worse than that silly Quins business and make scientific study even more difficult than it is with them. I thought, and I still think, that the way to learn about young Ted was to study him in his natural setting and not in a three-ring circus of advertisers and publicity men. So I laid myself out to play the whole thing down and keep it as quiet as possible.

'It wasn't as difficult as you might think to work that. Ada Filler was anxious to co-operate; her fear lest the neighbours should think there was anything "queer" about him was a great help. Jim wasn't awkward either. If he had been unemployed it would have been different, but he had a decent job and enough sense to see that, although there might be a bit of money in it, once the thing was known young Ted would become of public interest and virtually pass out of his parents' control.

'" "Ave to 'appen one day, I s'pose," was his opinion, "but the later the better, both for 'im and 'is mother, I say."

'More of a problem was young Ted himself. The most likely source of leakage was a child's natural desire to show off before other children. Luckily, when he did try it later, chance so arranged things that he was unconvincing and merely gained a discouraging reputation among his friends as a liar. That didn't matter, nearly all children boast and expect it of others, sometimes they believe one another, more often and without resentment, they don't.

'The first necessity seemed to me to give him a more efficient means of shielding himself from electrical influences than the one he had discovered. It was clear from his behaviour that his sense organs were always open to them, as one's ears are to sound, but with much more troublesome results. For the purpose I cut a strip of copper foil, padded it on one side and covered the other with brown cotton, with the idea that he might wear it as a kind of broad fillet. Experimentally there was a wire lead from it with a clip at the end, for it appeared likely that the screen might work better if it were earthed.

'I took the contraption round the following evening and let him try it on. The results were as good as I hoped; with an earth connection the radio influence was almost entirely screened off. It acted, one might say, as the eyelid of his new sense.

'Later, I developed a variation on it for daytime use. The fillet was hidden under a cap, and wires running down inside his clothes were attached to metal tips on his boots. This, he found, had considerable damping effect; if he could put his feet on a wet surface the screening was almost complete. The device became particularly useful later when he went to school. I supplied a certificate stating that, owing to a sensitive condition of the skull, it would be necessary for him to wear a cap indoors; but for this, I think he would have found concentration against the distractions which poured in on him difficult, if not impossible.

'When I set myself to learn what I could about young Ted's sensory experiences I very soon found myself engaged on a harder task than I had bargained for. Imagine yourself born blind and trying to understand the power of sight, or born deaf and being told about sound and music, and you'll begin to see something of what I was up against. Add the fact that your only source of information is an infant—extremely precocious in speech and understanding, it is true, but with an infant's wandering interest—and that no words exist to express his sensations except in terms of other senses, and progress is understandably slow.

'Nevertheless, I made some headway and began to form some hazy conceptions of the world his sixth sense showed him. It seemed to me that the new organs were somehow interconnected with the centres of vision and hearing, not like smell and taste, but more after the fashion of touch and hearing—you know how you can both feel and hear a deep note.

'For instance, he did not care to go very near the high-tension pylons. He complained sometimes that they were "too loud" and sometimes that they were "too bright." The perception itself seemed to partake of the nature of both. There was no occlusory device, so that, like his ears, the new organs were always on duty, yet, like eyes, they were capable of a kind of focus.

'The analogy which gradually built itself up in my mind was something like this. Imagine a man standing on a hilltop. Around him in every direction—and he can see in every direction at once—is a vivid, almost glaring, landscape. He can focus on any detail of the landscape and see it clearly amid the rest whenever he likes, but focused or not, he cannot help looking, for his eyes are fixed open.

'Or sometimes I would think of a man surrounded by all the intentional and unintentional instruments of noise; the sound waves beat at him incessantly, but he can pick out certain instruments if he tries. That, however, is a poorer analogy, for the boy's "electro-sentient" organs had a much greater power of discrimination than the human ear has.

'I'm afraid I can only convey poorly what I very dimly perceived myself, but I hope you can catch the idea to some extent. One was so hampered by lack of words and the looseness of meaning in those that had to be used. One continually ran up against things like this. It was clear enough that whatever Ted's system of reception of radio, his cognition made it intelligible to him as music and speech just as our auditory system does for us, but if one took him close to a transmitter, as I did experimentally, he complained that the broadcasting was "too bright."

' "You mean too loud," I suggested.

'But no. He wouldn't have that at all. For him it was "too bright."

'I don't want to bore you with technicalities and detailed accounts of my findings. That sort of thing is for the experts; I've got volumes of notes at home which I shall publish one day for them to scratch their heads over. More patience went into those than I have ever put into anything. I had to grasp each little hint and be ready to return to it later as the boy grew, for it was no good trying to force description and explanation before he was sufficiently developed to understand what I asked him. That sort of treatment produces, as I expect you know from experience, only a defiant sulkiness.

'Very often it was no good putting a question flatly. One had to set the scene and observe results. For instance, I had discovered that for him telegraph wires were alive, "lighted" he called it, with their electric messages. But it was no good putting the general question which occurred to me as a natural corollary: "Can you overhear telephone conversations?" He had probably never noticed whether he could or not—try asking the average child about overtones or the composition of a shade of colour. One had to take him close to a telephone wire and inquire the result. Actually the result was positive. He could "overhear" up to a distance of ten feet or so from the wires though he found it "faint."

'There were plenty of other discoveries. He knew at once whether an electric wire was "live" or not. The current he seemed to perceive perhaps as a fluid stemmed by the gap in the circuit. The radiation from cars with magnetos worried him, coil ignition bothered him only a little. He could judge voltages in wires with astonishing accuracy up to about 500 volts. Above that he found them all "bright."

'He had a high sensitivity, too, to static electricity, so much so that in certain weather nothing could induce him to brush or comb his hair, and, perhaps as a side issue of this, he showed a power of weather prediction some degrees more accurate than his elders'.'

CHAPTER FIVE

VOICES OF THE VOID

'By the time young Ted was ten and a half Jim had come to accept his son's powers as a permanent quality and not, as he had half suspected before, something which would be outgrown with childhood. He began to make plans for him. More impressed, perhaps, by the means of Ted's first self-revelation than by any of its subsequent manifestations Jim had ambitions to get him into the best wireless shop in Irkwell when he should leave school at fourteen.

' "That's the thing," he said. "Just let 'em try 'im once, that's all. Why 'e can tell where any set's wrong in a jiffy—and put it right, too. There's good money in a wireless shop, if a man knows the job, which most of 'em don't, seemingly. The lad ought to do well—maybe get a better job in one of the big places in Derby in a year or two."

'He looked disappointed when I shook my head.

' "What's wrong wi' that?" he demanded.

' "Not good enough, Jim," I told him. "What he ought to have if it can be managed is a real training. He'd just be wasting his time in a shop."

' "What, a college trainin' like? Seems to me like that's more like wastin' 'is time than t'other. If t'lad can do a job and 's a chance, let 'im do it, I say. There's plenty o' chaps full of book learnin' an' unemployed with it."

' "Ted wouldn't be," I said. "You don't realise it, Jim. This gift makes him something altogether exceptional. There's no telling where it may lead. Have you ever seen him examine a wireless valve? The contempt he has for it! He looks at it as you or I might look at a car without springs. I took him to a hospital once to show him the apparatus; he looked at all the radiography stuff and the rest of the electrical set-up the same way.

' "You see, Jim, all our most advanced electrical appliances seem quite primitive to him. Before long he'll begin to improve them. I tell you, Jim, I'm as certain of it as I ever was of anything in my life that he's going to revolutionise our conceptions and use of electricity. Once he gets going we're going to learn more in a few years than we've learned in the hundred and fifty since Volta made his battery. I can't see, no one can see, what changes he may bring about. Not just here, Jim, not just in England, but all over the world. It's going to be tremendous, I know it. And it's up to us to see that he has the best start we can give him."

'I think now that I made a tactical error in putting it to him like that. It might have been better if I had taken his own ideas for Ted and worked him up to broader views by degrees. Sprung on him like that, it just didn't register properly. In his own mind he probably put it down as a crazy idea. A suggestion that the boy might become locally important would have carried more weight. He shook his head.

' "Tha knows there's no money to send our Ted to college, Doctor."

' "Not much difficulty in raising it for a boy like him," I said.

' "What, borrow on the chance of 'is payin' it back when 'e 'ad a job? 'Oo's goin' to lend like that—'e might never 'ave a job, there's plenty as 'asn't; then what?"

' "No fear of that."

' "You can say so, but you can't be sure. I don't like it. I've always paid my way and owed nobody owt. It'd be a fine thing if I was to borrow for the lad and leave 'im to find t'money to pay back. Might take 'im years. 'Amperin' not 'elpin', that'd be. No, 'e shall 'ave the best I can give 'im, but what I can't, 'e shan't 'ave; and that's flat.'

'And flat it remained. No amount of reasoning or argument did anything but confirm him in what to his eyes was the decent, self-respecting course. When at last I was forced to recognise the hopelessness of converting him I tried to tell myself that in the long run it would make little difference—a bit more slogging, more time wasted in beginning, but the same later on—yet at the back of my mind I knew that wasn't the whole thing.

'Young Ted developed well, with all his father's sturdiness, a good share of the local commonsense outlook, and an amiable enough disposition. He held his place easily at school, not, I think, because his brain was anything but average, but because it was still in advance, though to a less extent, of his years. He got on well enough with the others and was frequently to be seen roving the town as a member of a gang of his own age or playing with them in the Irkwell Urban District Gardens. One was glad that, superficially, his interests seemed quite dully normal.

'In his eleventh and twelfth years, when I had feared he might want to forsake my company entirely for that of his gang, I still managed to see quite a lot of him—largely because he liked to come out in my car, I fancy—and it was when he was nearly twelve that I got a hint of something which bowled my imagination over.

'We were out late. My car had run a big-end up on the moors miles from anywhere. We had reached a main road and at last succeeded in getting a lift part of the way home, but we were left with five miles to cover and only our feet to carry us. It was a fine summer night and about as warm as it ever is on top of the hills. We had been going for some twenty minutes when Ted took off his cap and with it the copper shield which he wore concealed in the lining.

' "It's stopped," he said.

'I knew without asking that he meant that the B.B.C. middle and long-wave stations had closed down, and most of the powerful foreigners, too.

' "After midnight, then," I said.

' "Aye."

'We trudged on without speaking for a while. I knew that he was ranging about that queer electrical landscape of his, aware of things I should never know. And never had I been so—well, so jealous, I suppose it was, of his power as I was at that moment. Just then I felt that I would have given anything that could be asked of me just for a glimpse of the world through his sixth sense—just a glimpse, no matter how brief, so that I could begin to *understand*.

'He was at ease now. He complained these days that when the big stations were on, they were too loud so that they "dazzled" him unless he wore a shield, just as he complained that electric sparks hurt him like a very loud noise "only brighter-like." I knew that was so for I had seen him wincing painfully on account of a quite distant thunderstorm. I found myself suddenly and irrationally angry with him for having this extra world open to him and being unable to convey it to me.

'It was he who broke the silence and with it my unreasonable mood. He raised his hand and pointed upwards.

' "What's out there, Doctor?"

'I looked into the star scattered blue-black sky.

' "Space," I said. "Emptiness, or nearly, with little suns and planets floating about in it."

' "Aye, Mr. Pauley learned me that at school. But he didn't say owt about what goes on out there."

' "Goes on?"

' "Aye, goes on. 'E said as they was worlds, maybe like this, some of 'em, but nowt about t' chaps as lives on 'em, and what they do there."

' "He couldn't very well. You see, we don't even know that anyone does. Some people think that there may be life in some forms where conditions allow it, but others, the majority, think it unlikely."

' "They're daft."

' "Which of them?"

' "The ones as don't think so."

'I looked at him. His head was thrown back and his up-turned face shone dimly white in the starlight. A rush of excitement, almost physically painful, made my heart thump.

'It was hard to make my voice anything like normal as I asked:

' "Why?" and hung on his answer.

' "Why! Because if it ain't chaps like us doin' things out there, 'oo is it?"

'I did not dare to respond for a moment. From long experience I knew that at any display of excitement he took refuge in suspicious self-protection. Young Ted couldn't be driven, only led cautiously.

' "It wouldn't be God, would it?" he suggested hopefully.

'I told him I considered it unlikely.

' "What is it? Voices?" I added, as if out of a mild interest.

' "No. It's like—oh, like colours or notes."

' "Music?"

' "No, and 'tain't like any of the ordinary things, either. I'd know as it were different even if it weren't a long way away like it is."

'It took some time as usual to discover what he was meaning, but I had the impression at last that it was a thing happening at the far limits of his extra sense. As one cannot see stars in daylight, so he could perceive this disturbance only when the more powerful stations were off the air. It was something, it seemed, which happened in three tones. Tones of what? Something which was neither sound nor colour. They occurred in some deliberately arranged sequence—he was emphatic that they could not be accidental—yet they did not exactly repeat. They were faint and far away. He knew, knew without doubt, that they meant something, yet he couldn't tell what it was.

' "Like a chap gabbin' foreign," he tried, "you know as it means summat, but you don't know what. Like that, only different," he added with fair lucidity.

'And as different from accidental influences as "singin' from a motor 'orn."

'It left me more confused than usual. At one time I would think he implied someone signalling in a three-tone code, analogous perhaps to the dots and dashes of Morse. At another, that it was a system of communication which his intelligence could not grasp, in much the same way that we cannot grasp insects' methods of communication.

'But of one thing I went home that night quite certain. Here was such a possibility as I had never suspected. Beside it, all my earlier discoveries which had seemed so important, became trifling. Contact, perhaps some day communication, with the planets!'

CHAPTER SIX

THE GIFT OF AGES

'I THOUGHT over it all the next day with a great desire to do nothing precipitate. A wrong move now, I felt, might have tremendous effects.

'But the main result was that my earlier conviction grew clearer and clearer as a necessity. Young Ted must have a good education—the best we could get for him. The job of making sense of those signals, if it were possible at all, was not going to be easy.

'To use a metaphor over again, he was in the position of a man who hears dots and dashes, realises they are rational, but has never heard of Morse and is ignorant of the language used—perhaps Ted would be up against a worse problem; a quite unsimilar, incomprehensible type of intelligence behind signs.

'A puzzle like that is going to take all the intelligence and knowledge that can be brought to bear on it. For Ted to attempt it without all the resources one could give him would be inviting discouragement and failure. It needed a mind trained to patience and the scientific approach, perceptive and yet plodding, a mind with tenacity of purpose.

'Perhaps you can't give a mind those characteristics, but at least you can give it the chance to acquire them, and hope for the best. It was a chance I determined that young Ted in some way must have.

'With my own mind fully made up I went to see Jim Filler next evening.

'I intended to press again for Ted's education, but not to bring out my new reason for its necessity save as a last resource. For now our positions were curiously reversed from those of eight years ago; then it was he who was afraid I would not believe him, now I was pretty certain of being unable to convince him of the further development.

'It had been an uncertain kind of day, and there were dark clouds piling up on the horizon and a thundery feeling in the air when I arrived. Jim was working in his garden, but he stuck his fork into the ground when he saw me and led the way into the cottage.

'It wasn't difficult for him to guess what I'd come about. He was pretty used to my tackling him on the education issue by this time, though we never got any further, but this time the opening was easier than usual. It was, in fact, volunteered.

' "I've been thinkin' it over about our Ted," he said, "an' I don't know as it'll do 'im any 'arm to learn a bit, even if it don't do 'im no good."

' "Good," I said, feeling a bit taken aback at the complete *volte face.* "I was going to mention it."

' "Y' don't say," he answered drily.

' "I'm glad, very glad indeed," I went on, "I'm sure you'll

never regret it, nor Ted either. Well, now we'll have to go into
the matter of raising the money."

'He shook his head.

' "No, we won't. I said as 'ow I wasn't borrowin' for 'im, and
I ain't."

' "But—well, it's going to cost a bit, you know," I told him.

' "I know. I've been into all that."

'I waited. Jim's sort takes its own time.

' " 'E'll earn it 'imself. Maybe it'll take 'im a year or two, but
then 'e'll be able to go to college an' pay 'is own way."

' "How?"

'Jim chuckled.

' "Way you never thought of. Mr. Pauley's notion, an' a
good one, too."

'I had known that it must come; it was surprising that I had
had the field to myself for so long, yet I felt a hot resentment.

' "Pauley, where does he come in?" I asked, though I knew
on the moment exactly where he came in. It was inevitable
that someone should find out about young Ted soon, and who
likelier than his schoolmaster.

' "Same way as thaself. 'E came 'ere sayin' same as you, as 'ow
our Ted ought to go to college. So I tells 'im just t'same as I
tells you. Aye, an' I tells 'im it's no good 'im tryin' to change
my mind, seein' as you been tryin' to for t'best part of two
years, and not done it. So 'e goes off. Next day 'e's back. 'E's
been thinkin', 'e 'as. 'E says why not let our Ted go on t'Alls
and make a bit o' money 'imself?"

' "The Music Halls?"

' "Aye. 'E says a friend of 'is could get Ted on as "The
'Uman Wireless Set." Might make five quid a week and more."

'I thought of the plans I had made for the boy, a good
school and then Cambridge if it could be managed—and now,
"T'Alls!"

' "Jim," I said earnestly. "You can't do this. He can't afford
it, man, he's too important. He can't afford to spend the most
impressionable years of his life in Music Halls, it'd be the ruin
of him. How could he settle down to learn after that kind of
life? And he must learn, he's got to study, as hard as he can, he
must."

'Jim removed his pipe and looked hard at me.

' " 'Oo says 'e must? 'E's my own lad, isn't 'e? I got a right to
do what I think best for 'im, ain't I?"

' "But you don't understand, Jim, this is important, tremen-
dously important. It may mean a major turning point in his-

tory, Jim, pivoting on him. It's like a sacred trust, we must do our best to prepare him for it."

'I told him of my new discovery about Ted. I put my case for all I was worth—and I might as well have shouted at the hills. I could see his face harden into the all-too-familiar lines of obstinacy as I talked. He could not, would not, see, even if he believed. The stupendousness of the possibilities, contact with life beyond the Earth, perhaps knowledge from older, wiser worlds, the coming of a stage when man gropes out from the isolation of his little planet and makes himself known in the universe beyond, the importance to science, to mankind itself; all this was wasted, blunted against his conviction that it wasn't "right to borrow on t'lad's future."

'Because I felt so deeply, and partly because the coming storm made the air sultry and fretted the nerves, I lost my temper with him. But it would take more than words and threatening thunder to move Jim. Cloddish, without imagination, the embodiment of all the stupidities that clutter and clog the world, he seemed to me then.

'He wouldn't get excited, he refused to argue, he just sat there behind his unassailable rectitude, beating me off with flat negatives. No lash I used could sting him out of his quiet, narrow assurance. He just waited patiently for me to finish. I did that suddenly, for I felt that in another minute I should punch his silly face if only to make him come alive.

' "I'm going to see Pauley," I told him, "and I hope to Heaven that he at least has enough brains to see that this mustn't be allowed to happen. God, to waste the gift of the ages in a Music Hall!"

'I flung out of the place and across the pavement to my car. I was going to see the schoolmaster right away; perhaps he would believe easily, perhaps he would need convincing, but either way I could not believe that he would fail to see that Ted was going to deserve the best education possible. We might be able to raise the money as a gift, though I had my doubts whether Jim would accept it now. But somehow or other we must ensure Ted's—not only Ted's; the whole world's—chance.

'And then a rumble of thunder made me pause with my hand on the door handle. I looked up, suddenly aware that the sky was full of ominous black clouds; they looked fantastically heavy with an evil, almost green light in their caverns.

'That was why I did not rush off to see Pauley then; afterwards it wasn't necessary. . . .

'The threat of the thunder brought young Ted vividly into my mind. I knew how storms worried him, I knew, too, that he was not at home. I hesitated. After my exit I could scarcely go back and ask where he was; besides, Jim could hardly fail in the circumstances to misconstrue my motive, which was, in fact, merely a desire to be sure that the boy was as well protected as possible against an electrical upset. Instead, I turned from the car and spoke to the woman who stood in the doorway of the next cottage studying the sky resentfully.

'"Young Ted Filler?" she said. "Aye, 'e's along t'canal with our Rosie. Fair soaked they'll be, the pair of 'em."

'I remembered Rosie; she was one of those children who get themselves remembered. She was suspected, and not without reason, of being concerned in any bit of trouble for streets around.

'Even now I don't quite know why I changed my mind and went to look for young Ted instead of for Pauley, but I did.

'The canal ends in Irkwell so there was only one way to go. A few minutes later I stopped the car on a hump-backed bridge just as the first big drops of rain began to fall. From there I had a view of the towpath for half a mile each way, but I didn't need it. The path was deserted save for two small figures a hundred yards or so away; any others who may have been there had wisely left to seek shelter.

'The children were scuffling on the cinders a yard or two from the water's edge, much too occupied to pay attention to me, the coming storm, or anything else but their own quarrel. Rosie was no silent scrapper; her yells of protest were forceful even at that distance. Perhaps that was not to be wondered at. It must be painful to have an opponent take a good grip of one's hair, even if one does manage to get in a hack or two on his shins. I leaned out of the car and shouted at the little brutes.

'"Ted," I called, "stop it and come here."

'Surprised, he looked round. The victim seized her chance to pull free. Quick as a flash she snatched his cap off, flung it into the water, and tore off down the towpath with screams of derision.

'Ted clapped both hands to his head, as if in pain.

'"Come here," I shouted, getting out of the car.

'He heard me, for he turned and began to run with his hands still pressed to his head.

'I started off the bridge to get down to him, then I saw him stagger and stop. In the same split second came a vivid flash right above us and a crash of thunder like the end of the world. The rain fell as if a cloud had ripped right open. When I reached the towpath young Ted was lying there, pathetically asprawl and soaked through already.'

He paused.

'That's all,' he said, 'that was the silly end of it.'

We looked out over the dark lake in silence for a while.

'He was dead?' asked one of the Americans, at last.

'No, he wasn't dead. But the thing that made him different was dead. That terrific discharge of lightning had finished his sixth sense for good. In that new sense he had gone as blind as a man without eyes, as deaf as one with split eardrums. He came round again, an ordinary little Irkwell urchin, with a raging headache. Now, he's a quarryman like his father.

'Some day perhaps he'll do something silly and I shall be able to have a look at his brain—if his pigheaded relatives allow it. But there's pretty cold comfort in that when one thinks of the possibilities which were snuffed out in a second.'

No one spoke again for some minutes. Then there was a movement in the darkness from the Lancashire·man's direction.

'Aye, it were a rum do,' he said, 'but 'e'll be 'appier that way, you know. Freaks ain't 'appy. Now, there was one as I once talked to at Blackpool. 'E wasn't 'appy, 'e said. . . .'

THE LAST LUNARIANS

CHAPTER ONE

THE VOYAGE OF THE *SCINTILLA*

THE secretary of the Lunar Archaeological Society approached his employer with a nervous diffidence. His method of stating his business was, to put it mildly, indirect. The president was a man who hated circumlocution. He became testy.

'Come on, man. What's the trouble? Out with it!'

Still the secretary hesitated, then, with a sudden decision, thrust a packet of papers clumsily towards his chief.

'These came this morning, sir. I thought you ought to know. They're a bit—er—peculiar.'

'All right. I'll look at 'em.'

The secretary departed with some relief, and the president turned back to his interrupted work. Half an hour later, he remembered the pile of papers and took up the covering letter which lay on top.

A name standing out amid the type caught his eye. He stiffened, stared at it and began to read more carefully. The heading was a Liverpool address, and the date a fortnight old.

'Dear Sir,' it began. 'On the sixteenth of June last, the S.S. *Turkoman*, to which I was medical officer, rescued a man at a point not far from the Solomon Islands. He was found drifting in a native canoe and, judging from his condition, had been in it for some days. The results of such exposure were aggravated by the serious ill-treatment he had received in the form of severe cuts and wounds. At first it appeared to be impossible to save him, but his body eventually responded to treatment, though his mind still wandered.

'He was a man of considerable education, and gave his name as Stephen Dawcott. Upon arrival here, I placed him in a mental home. During the next four months I was absent, and when I returned, it was to find that he had made good his escape. The authorities were mystified and handed to me the enclosed manuscript, which he had left behind. They saw it as the raving of a madman, but to me it seems a matter requiring a less facile explanation. I await your reply with interest.'

The signature was 'John Haddon,' and to it were appended the letters, 'M.D.'

The president frowned as he set aside the letter and took up the manuscript. There had been a Stephen Dawcott, an anthropologist of some note, aboard the *Scintilla*. But the *Scintilla* was lost. From the day she had left the flying field on her maiden trip to the Moon, nearly a year ago. not a word had been heard from her. She had roared from Earth into mysterious non-existence.

But Stephen Dawcott had been aboard her; he was sure of that. He, and others of the Lunar Archaeological Society, had seen Dawcott's among the faces at the windows before the *Scintilla* took off. And now the man was reported as having been picked up in Melanesia, of all unlikely places. The president's frown deepened as he began to read the manuscript: —

The *Scintilla* behaved in an exemplary manner on her outward journey. She justified the high hopes of her designers by the smooth swiftness with which she leapt out from Earth. Captain Tott was delighted with her performance, and swore that there could be no sweeter ship to handle in all the ether.

Those of us who had taken part in earlier space-flights agreed unreservedly. The new Danielson acceleration compensators had proved their worth, and ridded space-flying for evermore of the starting strain and its unpleasant effects. In design, furnishing, and facilities for carrying such fragile relics as we might find, the *Scintilla* was a credit to the Lunar Archaeological Society who had built and so lavishly equipped her.

The perfect start, followed by the peaceful smoothness of our voyage, could have raised no apprehensions in the most psychic soul. Indeed, what possible cause could there be for apprehension? The silver globe before us was worn out, arid and still with the supreme stillness of death. No ship cruising above that gutted shell of a world had seen sign of as much life as lies in a blade of grass. Even the crater of Linné, which had been suspected of harbouring the last vestiges of life, had been found as barren as the rest.

'Dead,' I murmured, as we gazed out of the living-cabin windows at the withered satellite. 'All the "fitful-fevers" done and gone; a whole world mummified and at rest.'

But I did not know Luna then. I did not know to the full that desperation with which life strives and clings. . . .

We made first for the North-East Quadrant, and sank to a gentle landing on the glittering, metallic dust which makes the crater of Aristarchus the brightest spot on the face of the Moon.

This was to be a preliminary trip. Our object was to survey the ground for future operations rather than make them ourselves. A number of sites were to be examined and reported upon, with a view to deciding which would be the most profitable to excavate. Aristarchus held little of interest for us, save the almost obliterated remains of a small settlement upon the northern side.

The details of our trip are of little interest here, so I merely record that we moved next, unprofitably, to the Mare Crisium, and thence across the equator to Tycho. Next, Clavius, greatest of all the craters, provided quantities of material, and showed indisputably that a great civilisation had once flourished in what is now only a vast bowl of sand and rock, a hundred and forty miles in diameter. Thus we came at last to the Mare Serenitatis, the Sea of Serenity. . . .

Who named this immense oval plain? I cannot remember, but I do know that he saw it only through a telescope, two hundred and thirty-nine thousand miles away. He did not see it as we did—a huge sterile stretch, grey-floored and gloomy. Had he been able to stand upon one of the tortured mountains at its brink and look out across that sombre desolation of sand, he would have called it, not the Sea of Serenity, but the Sea of Foreboding. . . .

We sailed slowly across to the North-West. Every member of the expedition was at the windows, scanning the featureless floor for any sign the ancient Lunarians might have left.

Until now we had felt no uneasiness. All the Moon is bare, but the harshness of its vistas had not played upon our nerves; it was only what we had expected and could scarcely affect us, but now the monotony of this great, dry sea-bed seemed to impress us all in greater or lesser degree. Unromantic scientists though we were, we felt a misgiving which none of us was willing to put into words.

And then, less than twenty miles from the far side of the sea, the steady throbbing of our rockets was interrupted. The firing tubes began to stutter uncertainly. I was with Captain Toft when the chief engineer rang through and reported that it would be necessary to descend for repairs.

The hasty glance which Toft gave through the control-dome windows told me that he had conceived the same distaste for the locality as had the rest of us. He decided swiftly to make for the cliffs now looming ahead at the sea's edge. There could be no better landing surface than the level, grey sand beneath us, but he preferred to stop near its confines. With some anxiety, he inquired the extent of the failure, but was told that this could not be ascertained while in flight.

The *Scintilla* continued to forge lamely ahead, gradually sinking. She took the sand at length some two hundred yards from those high, perpendicular cliffs which once had stood like the ramparts of giants against a beating sea.

The Captain left the dome to interview the engineer, and I made my way to the central saloon. A deal of chatter greeted me as I opened the door. My colleagues were peering excitedly at the cliffs; all signs of their depression had vanished. Robson, the leader of the scientific side of the expedition, drew me forward and thrust a pair of field-glasses into my hands.

'Look at those cliffs, man. Just look at them!'

I focused eagerly. The sand in the immediate foreground was dotted with rocks of all sizes which had fallen from the heights, and beyond them was a line of darkness which hid the cliff-face in deep shadow. The meagre, reflected light was just enough to show regular markings of some kind. I fancied that I could make out the carved figure of a man.

'Wait a minute,' cried Robson, as he turned and dashed from the room.

A moment later, a searchlight was playing a flood of brilliance on to a scene which caused us to gasp incredulously. The surface of the granite-like rock, to the height of some seventy or eighty feet, was covered with carvings in high relief —an involved, ingenious ordering of the figures of men, animals, and conventional forms.

The first astonished silence was succeeded by a babel of excited talk. Everyone spoke at once, and no one listened. And no wonder; compared to this revelation, our earlier discoveries dwindled to mere nothings. It seemed that we might have found the lunar Book of the Dead carved upon this mighty stone page.

CHAPTER TWO

CORPSES OF THE MOON

ROBSON came back and started to tow me in the direction of the space-suit lockers. He continued to babble excitedly as he lifted the clumsy garments from their hooks. The suits were essential, for although, contrary to expectation, it had been found that some air still existed upon the Moon, and in the deepest craters was almost breathable during the lunar day, yet the rarity of such as lingered in the beds of the vanished seas compelled artificial aid.

As we left the ship and drew near the cliffs, I think there was no doubt in any of our minds that the design was picture-writing of some kind. The irregular repetition of certain glyphs practically established the fact. None of us, of course, could yet attempt any translation, but the photographers were already arranging their cameras to provide a record for more leisured study.

I watched them work with an untraceable sense of uneasiness creeping over me. I have said before, and I repeat, that although I am a hard-headed scientist, I was nevertheless aware of a distinctly unscientific misgiving....

The rest were too enthusiastic, too occupied with pointing out details and symbols which might, or might not, be analogous with similar symbols on Earth, to share my anxiety; and I did not mention it—it was too irrational, illogical.

It was Robson who made the great find. He had gone close up to the cliff, and was examining a floridly incised square of the surface. Presently his cry sounded in all our receivers:

'A door,' he said. 'There's a door in the cliff!'

We crowded up to him and found that the square was bordered all around by a narrow crack. Millennia ago, when there had been a wind upon the Moon, the grey sand had drifted up at the foot, but it took only a few moments' scratching to lay bare the threshold of the stone panel. Already, at the ruins in Clavius, we had established that the luna practice had been to swing a door upon a central pivot so that it turned sidewise through ninety degrees, leaving a passage to either side.

Accordingly, Robson flung himself upon one side and pushed. Finding it immovable, he transferred his strength to the other. It moved back an inch or so and then stuck. Spurred on, he brought every once of his strength to bear, and slowly the great rock door, which would have defied the efforts of three men on Earth, swung around.

Without hesitation, he switched on the light at his belt and walked in. We followed him for ten yards; then he stopped.

'Another door,' he complained irritably. 'They certainly meant to preserve whatever's inside. Let's have some more light on this.'

The second door was plainer than the outer, and the only sign on it was a deep-graven circle. As I looked at that circle, my premonitions intensified. The circle—the world-wide sign of infinity, eternity—could it be possible that here, on Luna . . .?

I almost called upon the others to stop, but realised in time how weakly my warning would fall before their exploring zest.

'It's sealed,' someone discovered. He pointed to a dozen or more blobs of black, shiny composition fixed across the jambs. On each of these, too, was impressed the sign of the circle.

To the non-anthropologist, it may seem strange that I should have attached an Earthly importance to the sign of the circle here on the Moon. But it is, with the possible exception of the cross, the earliest and most widely used of symbols. It was significant of man's will to immortality in all parts of the globe from far back in pre-history and it remains significant still. It had dominated the lives of many races, and now here it was again—on the Moon!

I stood unhappily aside and watched the rest break the seals. But the door still refused to yield, even to the efforts of five men. They drew their knives and fell to scraping out a tight-plugged paste around the edges. They tried again, but still the stone square stood adamant.

Robson suggested a small charge of explosive. 'The door has no value,' he pointed out. 'There's no carving on it except the circle.' The rest agreed, after a momentary hesitation. Ten minutes later, the face of the door was cracked across, and a crow-bar was levering the fragments apart. The barrier soon succumbed, and we scrambled over the ruins to arrive in a large hewn room. Here and there, black openings in the walls suggested corridors to further rooms, but we gave them little attention at present, for our interest was centred in a scatter of long boxes lying on the floor.

They were made of some grey metal which reflected the rays of our lamps only dully. One, close by the door, had suffered from the explosion. The lid was loosened and lay awry. Through the space it had opened, there hung a human hand. . . .

Robson laid hold of the battered edge and wrenched the lid clean away. As his eyes fell on the contents, he started back in surprise. We hurried to his side and stared down in astonishment—men of Earth looking for the first time upon a man of the Moon!

He was perfectly preserved, and we, poor fools, wondered at the artistry which had been able so to conserve an unshrouded corpse that after thousands—perhaps millions—of years, it could have appeared to have lived but yesterday. Not one of us guessed the truth about that body. We were sufficiently conceited to believe that no race could have surpassed us in any branch of knowledge.

We looked down upon the Moonman, noting his almost unbelievable chest development; remarking his brown pigmentation and the Mongolian slant of his eyes; observing that he was a litle shorter than the shortest of us, and telling one another that he was brachycephalic; classifying him. If any one of us happened to notice that the lips were drawn back in a smile, he did not mention it—of what interest to a scientist is a dead man's smile . . . ?

When we returned to the *Scintilla* for rest and replenishment of our oxygen supplies, Captain Toft greeted us with the information that the wear in our firing tubes was more extensive than had been suspected. It would take, he thought, nearly twenty-four hours to effect the replacements.

The delay irritated him, for he had meant to follow daylight around the Moon to the invisible side. The present situation would cause night to overtake us, for the flaring Sun was already not far from the horizon, and the dark line of the two weeks long lunar night was crawling towards us, a bare twelve hours away.

But we did not share his anxiety to be off. Indeed, we welcomed the delay, for it gave us some time for investigation. Night or day would not matter to us in the rock vault.

A dozen specimen coffins were loaded aboard the *Scintilla*, after we had opened them to assure ourselves that they contained the bodies of six men and six women. With these safely stowed away, we felt at liberty to examine the vault more thoroughly.

There was little to repay detailed investigation of the place itself. No carving or decoration graced the interior, but we found that it and the subsidiary chambers contained a surprising quantity of coffins—altogether, more than four hundred of them.

Each one, when opened, revealed a puzzling device whose purpose we could not guess. As the lid was raised on its hinges, two secondary occurrences took place. At the first loosening of the catches, something inside dropped with a musical tinkle. Investigation revealed the fragments of a small glass globe, smashed to pieces. Then the actual pushing up of the lid thrust, by means of an ingenious arrangement of levers, a slender, hollow glass spike deep into the corpse's flank. This was automatically withdrawn as the lid passed the perpendicular.

Robson and I examined the device curiously, but could make nothing of it.

'I guess it's something to do with preservation,' he suggested vaguely, and turned his attention to the other contents.

CHAPTER THREE

FROM OUT OF THE PAST

MANY of the coffins enclosed not only trinkets and trappings upon the still forms, but also sheets of withered writing material covered with a quasi-pictorial script. This obviously must be collected, but since prolonged work in space-suits is inadvisable, we came to an arrangement of shifts. My turn came some six hours before sunset, and my companions were Jay Royden and Walter Greg, good men both.

We were not unduly depressed when we left the *Scintilla's* lock. My own earlier misgivings had all but disappeared under the cheering influence of the others, and if I thought at all, as we made for the vault entrance, it was of the good luck which had caused the *Scintilla* to have her misadventure here. But for that, we might never have seen the rock carvings.

The three of us were soon scrambling once more into the hewn tomb. For an hour or more we worked quietly. Necklaces, bangles, daggers and rings, which would soon be proudly shown in the museums of Earth, were methodically stripped from their owners' still forms. The Lunarians, it seemed, did not know clothes as we do. What little they wore was not for covering, but for ornament in the way of worked belts, intricate breastplates and the like.

Very soon our miscellaneous collection began to form a sizeable pile, and I decided that it would be more convenient to remove it from the chamber where we were working to a spot nearer the main entrance. Two journeys were necessary, and as I made the second, I came upon a sight which brought me up with a jerk. One of the coffins by my way lay open, and the inmate's hand rested on the edge....

I stared in shocked horror. It had not lain so during my previous journey. I hurried past with a thumping, painful heart. I dropped my burden with the other plunder, and turned to scan the vault with the awful intensity of growing panic.

My ears strained to listen, though I was cut off from all

external sounds. Something seemed to flicker just beyond the rays of my lamp. I jerked stiffly towards it, but the light showed nothing amiss. I turned on, scouring the place with my lamp. Nothing.... Nothing....

Then I looked back to the first corner. My arms fell weakly; my heart hammered in panic. A corpse sat upright in its coffin!

I must have cried out, for I heard Walter's voice in my receiver. 'What is it?' he was calling anxiously.

'Come here, quick,' was all I could manage.

The urgency in my voice started them without further question. I stood with my back to the main entrance and turned my light on the passage-mouth from which they must emerge. Something moved again outside the circle of light, but I dared not throw the rays upon it.

The two grotesque, space-suit-clad figures came hurrying into sight. As they saw me, Walter demanded again: 'What is it?'

I did not answer him; instead I shouted: 'Look out!' A dimly-seen shape was moving in the shadow behind them.

Walter snatched at his knife and made to turn, but swift as he was, he was too late.

A naked, brown arm came snaking over his shoulder. Its elbow crooked under the front of his helmet and dragged his head back. Another brown hand shot groping for his knife.

And even as Jay turned to help, another pair of brown arms came twining about him, and I had a glimpse of a slant-eyed face leering beyond.

The hand which sought Walter's knife tore it from his grasp. I could hear him grunt as he struggled to keep it. Then clearly through the microphone came a tearing sound, as the knife ripped the space-suit, and the following whistle of exhaling air. Walter gave one choking cry....

The whole affair had been too sudden for me to give any help. Before I could take more than a step, came a second tearing sound and I knew that Jay, too, was past help.

I stopped suddenly—no use to go on. Then I saw that the corpse which had caused my fright was no longer sitting—he was climbing out of his coffin, his face leering towards me....

I turned and sprang for the open, racing for my life across the sea-bottom.

They didn't believe it. Already I had shown signs of queer behaviour, and now I was babbling fantastic nonsense. Dead men coming to life! Dead men fighting the living! Obviously, my brain was turned.

The doctor attempted to soothe me. Robson vainly attempted to reach Walter and Jay on the radio. There was an odd expression on his face when he turned back to look at me.

'Can't raise them,' he said. 'Something's certainly wrong. Do you think——?' He broke off and nodded suggestively towards me. The rest looked serious. They did not put their thoughts into words, but they were plain enough on their faces. Three men alone—and one of them a madman!

Two volunteered to go out and search. The rest began to help them into their space-suits. I begged and besought them not to go, but they only cursed me for getting in their way. Others dragged me back and held me penned in a corner.

'Good God, you fools,' I raged at them, 'wouldn't they have called you if I'd run amuck like you think? Can't you see that I'm telling you the truth? If you go over there, they'll get you, you fools—you bloody fools! They'll get you!'

Nobody gave me a scrap of attention. The men were clad and their helmets affixed. As they left the air-lock, Robson switched on the radio to keep in communication. My anger passed as I helplessly watched them trudge towards the search-lit cliff-face. Nothing I could do would save them now.

We saw them pause by the open stone door and heard their voices in the speaker as they settled who should take the lead. Then they disappeared. For a few seconds there was nothing but the sound of breathing. Suddenly a voice with a tinge of nervousness spoke.

'What was that? Something moved.'

'Nothing,' answered the other. For our benefit, he added: 'We are just climbing over the remains of the second door—now we're in the vault. There's—God, what's that?'

His voice was suddenly shrill—and then it broke. 'Quick, out of this, quick, man—back, for Heaven's sake!' After that it was a jumble—hard breathing mingled with odd phrases. '—dozens of 'em.' '—got him.' 'Keep together.' Then: 'Look out, he's got a knife!' Horror-stricken, we heard the sound of stout cloth ripped asunder—gasping cries. After that, all was silent....

My companions turned wondering eyes upon me, full of uneasy fears. Robson murmured something which might have been an apology. He begged for the whole story. I told him as calmly as I could all that I knew.

He found it meagre. 'Have you any theories?' he demanded.

I had been thinking, but I hesitated. 'It's rather a fantastic theory,' I admitted.

'Of course it is! The whole thing's fantastic. Let's have it.'

'You remember what happened when we opened the coffins? A globe of something dropped and smashed. Then, too, there were those glass needles.... There must have been a purpose behind them.'

Robson looked hard at me. 'You mean that the needles might have been some kind of hypodermic?'

'Something of the sort,' I nodded.

'And that they revived what we thought were corpses?'

'There were the glass globes, too,' I reminded him.

'But it's ridiculous, preposterous! After thousands of years. ... There might be a possibility of suspended animation for a short time, but this . . .'

'Why should it be impossible for an indefinite length of time? The fact that we don't know how to do it doesn't prove its impossibility. Those coffins were air-tight; they may have been full of preserving gas, for all we know. We couldn't notice that while we were wearing space-suits.'

'But——'

'Oh, all right,' I said. 'I'm only offering a theory. Can you think of a better one?'

Robson turned to contemplate the cliff.

'But why?' he murmured. 'Why?'

'Why do men put up memorials?' I asked. 'It's a habit, an instinct to perpetuate. I should say these people had just the same instinct. Their world was dying; the race was dying. Perhaps they thought that it was only a phase and that the Moon would become fertile once more. Anyway, on the face of it, it looks as though they decided to take a chance and try to save some of their race for whatever future there might be.'

'But how can they live?' asked someone. 'There's hardly any air.'

'But remember the enormous lung capacity,' suggested Robson.

CHAPTER FOUR

BESIEGED BY THE MOON-MEN

WITH the suggestion of a rational explanation, the fears of the party grew less intense. Some of the more adventurous even volunteered to undertake a further investigation. They could go prepared and well armed.

Robson vetoed the idea at once. He pointed out that there were over four hundred Lunarians ready to over-run them faster than they could fire.

'But we don't mean them any harm.'

'Nor did the others, but they got theirs. It doesn't seem to have occurred to you that they must have food. There was nothing to eat in the vault.'

We looked at one another. This implication of the immediate capture of our men had not struck us before. It did so now, unpleasantly. . . .

Robson summoned Captain Toft. This was a danger which concerned the whole ship, not merely our scientific group.

The Captain's incredulity was easily beaten down by our massed conviction. He was all for action and rescue, until he realised that the space-suits had been slit and that the men were past all help. Robson pressed for the immediate removal of the *Scintilla* from the Mare Serenitatis to a less dangerous resting-place in some crater; but Toft shook his head.

'The engines are down for repairs. Even by forcing work to the limit, it'll take another ten hours.' Our faces looked anxious enough to make him add: 'I'll do my best, gentlemen, you may depend on that, but I can't promise a minute less than ten hours.'

Robson thought for a while. At last he spoke.

'We must keep them penned up as long as we can. I want two men to go outside and take rifles. Every man or woman who tries to get out of that vault must be shot.'

Two volunteers were immediately forthcoming. They hurried into space-suits, and were on their way to the lock when a shout from a watcher at the window stopped them.

'Too late.' he called. 'They're out!'

A knot of a dozen or more Moonmen had just emerged. They halted a few paces from the cliff and stood on the grey sand, shielding their eyes with their hands from the glare of our searchlight, and looking about them.

Now that they were erect, their differences from Earth-men appeared more pronounced. The large ears developed for catching sounds in the thin air seemed to dwarf their heads, and the huge bulging chests were so disproportionate as to render all the limbs skinny and spindly by contrast. They looked bewildered by the barrenness of the world they now faced. Not only did it fail to fulfil their expectations, but it was obviously different from their last view of it.

One man raised his arm and pointed to a distinctively dis-
torted crag, as though it were a recognisable landmark. The
rest nodded and let their eyes wander, searching for other
familiar sights. More of their kind came out of the vault and
joined them. After a short conference, they seemed to reach a
decision and the whole group turned towards the *Scintilla*.

The doctor, standing next to me, was watching them with
close attention.

'They're not doing too well,' he murmured. 'Even those
great lungs are labouring a bit. The atmosphere must have
been a great deal denser when they went in. I wonder just how
long ago——?'

Robson's voice cut him short. He was addressing the two in
space-suits.

'They mean mischief. You two get up into the control-dome
and take your rifles. We'll evacuate the dome, and then you
can open the windows and pick them off, if necessary.'

The two men left the room, and we heard them clattering
up the metal ladders. Robson was right. The Moonmen and
women did mean mischief. It was in their gleaming eyes and
bared teeth as they approached.

They had resumed the trappings that we had pilfered. Each
wore the broad worked belt of Luna, and about their necks
and ankles glittered metal bangles. Black hair, held back from
their faces by ornate circlets, depended in a lank mane upon
their shoulders and down their backs.

One man, slightly taller than the rest, appeared to be the
leader. As they drew close, he turned to incite the rest. A
moment later, a volley of rocks and stones clattered futilely
against the *Scintilla's* metal sides.

We took heart. The primitive simplicity of such an attack
encouraged us. Half a minute later, two Moon-men dropped
inert. Our men in the dome had gone into action. The attackers, by now a hundred strong, were thrown into momentary confusion. But the wavering was brief, and in a few seconds, they were running towards us. They had seen in a flash
that once beneath the ship's overhanging sides, they would be
safe from the marksmen above.

A well-placed rock put the searchlight out of action and
plunged the cliff-face into intense shadow. It became impossible for the riflemen to pick off the reinforcements which
would pour from the tomb. They would be all but invisible
until the line of sunlight was reached—and that line was crawling slowly closer to us with the sinking of the Sun.

Another searchlight was switched on, but it, too, was swiftly obscured. The main body of the attackers was now out of view from our windows, though a large number of stragglers continued to dart from the shadow towards the ship. Of these, a number fell to the guns, but a larger number won through unharmed.

From down the corridor came the sudden clanging of an attack upon our outer door. We looked at one another and smiled. There was precious little to be feared from that direction. Nor were the Moon-men long in realising that the steel would defy their utmost efforts. In a very short time, they came clustering around the window, hungrily gloating and excitedly jostling one another as they peered in.

The leader picked up a prodigious rock which could not have been stirred by one man on Earth. He flung it with a mighty heave against the fused pane. The pane was unharmed, but Robson looked serious.

'I don't know how much of that sort of thing it will stand,' he said doubtfully. 'If they try two or three of those rocks simultaneously——?'

The same idea had occurred to the Moon-men. We saw them collecting the largest rocks they could handle. There was a leering look of triumph on the face of the leader as he regarded us through his slant eyes.

Robson rushed back and opened the door. 'Quick, out of this!' he shouted.

We left in a headlong rush, and as the last of us came through, we heard the crash of the shattered window. The door snapped to behind us automatically as the air pressure fell.

Within a couple of minutes, a furious battering began towards the stern. Half a dozen of us raced down the ship. As we clattered through the engine-room, the chief engineer looked up, spanner in hand. He was working all he knew. The grime on his face was trickled with sweat and his hair lay damp and flat.

'Clamp on the emergency plates,' he called as we passed.

There had been no time in the main cabin to fix the heavy steel plates across the windows, but now we seized them from their racks and set to with a will. No sooner was a plate fixed over one port-hole than the Moon-men turned their attack to another, and we had to rush that also to cover with an emergency plate.

In the middle of our activity came word that the men in the control-dome were abandoning their position. The place was becoming untenable on account of the bombardment of rocks, for while the rocks could be thrown on a trajectory which kept the throwers concealed, the riflemen must have direct vision before their shots could be effective.

For what seemed several hours, we lived in a nightmare of rushes from point to point. As fast as we made one spot safe, another was attacked. Then, at last, when we were weary to the point of exhaustion, we became aware that the frenzy was lessening. The batterings grew fewer and feebler, until at length they stopped altogether.

We waited, puzzled. It was almost an hour before we cautiously removed an emergency plate and peered out. Only then did we understand the abrupt cessation of hostilities. The Sun had set, and the sea-bed shimmered coldly in the pale, green-blue Earth-light. Of the Moon-men, only a few still, crumpled forms were to be seen.

'They've gone,' I said. 'But why?'

Robson pointed towards the cliff, and I saw that the stone door was now closed.

'The cold,' he explained. 'Right now it's colder out there than anything you've ever known. In a little while, it will be so cold that what little air there is left will freeze solid.'

'And the Moon-men?'

'It means the end of them. Even in their vaults, the air will freeze—though they'll freeze first.'

'Poor devils,' I said. 'To wait all those thousands of years just for this—to freeze to death!'

I had an unhappy vision of the last luckless Moon-men and women huddled together in their lightless tomb, waiting without hope for the creeping coldness of death. Robson's voice broke my mood.

'All hands on the job,' he said briskly. 'We've got to get ship-shape again. Captain Toft, what are your orders, sir?'

CHAPTER FIVE

THE TWELVE COFFINS

It was decided that we would make for Earth. The morale of the *Scintilla*'s company was too shaken to undertake the exploration of Luna's hidden side on our present trip. Since little or no calculation was necessary, Toft waited only until the engines were repaired before he headed straight for the great pale disc of Terra.

The ground fell away, and we looked for the last time on that misnamed Sea of Serenity. A few scattered brown figures were visible in the Earth-light; they seemed like a sad symbol of the littleness of that passing phase of worlds which we call life. With that final glimpse, those of us not on duty turned away and sought our cabins for overdue rest.

I slept long. It was all of twelve hours before I reopened my cabin door. My way down the passage led me past the chief engineer's room, and I hesitated outside his door, wondering whether to take him along for breakfast or whether to let him have his sleep out. My hand was on the knob when the door opened abruptly and in the doorway stood a woman—a Moon-woman!

I stood frozen with the shock, staring at her. She returned the stare, white teeth and dark eyes glinting. She crouched slightly, becoming the more grotesque and horrifying. Her right hand slid forward, and I saw that it held a knife which was red with blood.

I lunged to grip her wrist, but she was too swift. With a twist and a cry, she had passed me and was away up the corridor. I hesitated, then turned into the engineer's cabin. One look at him was enough; that Moon-devil must have slashed and slashed. . . .

For a moment I stood irresolute. The engineer's fate might well have been mine—and I was not safe now. I ran into the corridor; the rest must be warned.

At the threshold of the living-cabin, I checked in horror. Five still forms lay on the floor, each of them horribly mutilated. I recoiled and fled to the control-dome, hoping desperately.

My fears were not vain. Just in the entrance, I stumbled over the bodies of two officers. Beside a third figure crouched a Moon-woman. At my entrance, she arose and whirled towards me; I could see that the man at her feet was Toft, alive, but bound and helpless.

She faced me like some terrifying Medusa, stepping cat-like, a knife in either hand. I backed and grasped a chair, intending to use it as a weapon—I had forgotten that all furniture on the ship must be fixed. She gave a cry, semi-human and chilling. A door on the far side of the dome opened suddenly to reveal a group of the grotesque Moon-men and women.

It was more than I could stand; I fled, bolting the door behind me.

For the next twelve hours, I remained locked in my cabin. There was plenty of time to review our folly. How could we, even in our excitement, have overlooked the possibility of menace from those twelve coffins that we had taken aboard? And not only had we taken them aboard, but we had even opened them to assure ourselves of their contents. Surely, some of us should have foreseen the danger! Either Robson or myself ought to have fastened down the lids, or, better still, have jettisoned them upon the Moon.

And in the middle of my self-blame, it came to me that this was not the end. They must have taken the ship completely by surprise and murdered every man they had found except Toft; they would make him show them how to work the ship, or else force him to guide the *Scintilla* back to Earth himself. The Moon-people had planned thousands of years ago their bid for survival, and it had not yet failed. A dozen of the Lunarians might yet be let loose upon Earth.

I was unarmed, for all the weapons were kept in a cupboard off the main living-cabin. I would have to get there before I could avenge my comrades and wipe out the Moon-folk. I crept to the door and listened. One hasty glance up and down the corridor assured me that it was empty, and I made stealthily in the direction of the bows.

I reached the main cabin undetected, and slipped inside. Averting my eyes from the shambles on the floor, I sought the armoury cupboard. Its steel door was locked. . . .

Footsteps rang on the floor beyond the opposite door. In a flash, I was across the room and back by the way I had entered —weaponless, and perhaps the only survivor, unless they had permitted Toft still to live. What could I do? I could think of nothing but that I must live and carry my warning. And to live, I must have food.

By devious ways I gained the store-room, and piled the necessities of life into an empty case. I had lugged it half-way back to my cabin when misfortune overtook me. Rounding a corner, I came face to face with a Moon-man.

His surprise was greater than mine—I got in a good drive to the chin while he still stared. He went down with a cry which was half shout and half groan. It was not loud, but it served to alarm his fellows. There came a din of feet pounding down the corridor behind me. Leaving my case of food, I jumped over the prostrate man and fled.

Running and sliding on the metal floors, I made for the only safe place I knew; my cabin. The clatter of pursuing feet grew louder, spurring me on. Turning at last into the final alley, I found my way blocked. But I was desperate, and there was only one thing to do. I put my head down and charged like a bull at the four brown figures before me.

There was a brief, whirling nightmare of kicking and hammering, and then somehow I broke out of that mêlée and gained my cabin. With a final effort, I slammed the door in my pursuers' faces. My chest and face were bloody and lacerated. I remember pulling free a Moon-man's dagger which lodged in my left shoulder; and after that—nothing. . . .

The jolt of a rough landing finally roused me from my sleep or coma. With an excruciating effort, I raised my stiff body to look through the small port-hole. Outside was a stretch of white sand and beyond it a line of frothing breakers, glistening in the sunlight. Somehow, the Moon-men had brought the *Scintilla* back to Earth.

I was a sick man, and it took me a long time to move. When at length I managed to stagger down the passage, it was to find the entrance wide open and the ship deserted. Somewhere in the green forest which fringed the beach, the Moon-folk were prowling and hunting.

I made my difficult way to the fuel-store, and close to the tanks I lit a slow fuse; at least there would be no *Scintilla* as a safe base for the Moon-devils' operations. Then, as fast as I could, I made my way along the shore.

A few days later, I found a long-neglected canoe. I repaired it the best I could and paddled it out to sea.

The President of the Lunar Archaeological Society frowned. He pulled his ear reflectively, and shook his head slowly. He turned the bunch of papers over and, still frowning, began to read them again.

Preposterous, of course, but—well, there *had* been a Stephen Dawcott, and he *had* sailed on the *Scintilla*. . . .

THE PUFF-BALL MENACE

THE Prince Khordah of Ghangistan was in a bitter mood. His council, seated cross-legged upon a semi-circle of cushions before him, had come to know too well that look of dissatisfaction. Of late it had seemed to dwell perpetually upon his dark features. The members of the council were aware of his words before he spoke, so often had they heard them.

'To all great nations,' he observed, 'might is right. Today we hear much talk of the rights of small nations—and to what does it amount? Nothing but so much dust in the wind to fill the eyes of those who would see.'

He glowered upon his councillors. Each appeared occupied in an interested study of the mosaic floor; the beauty of its patterns was more soothing than the expression on the Prince's face. More than one grimy forefinger scratched in its owner's beard in order to give a misleading suggestion of thought.

The council was formed entirely of old men. Not that old men are always wise, but they do have the advantage of less fiery ambition, and, whether one is a Prince in Ghangistan, or a Big Shot in Chicago, too much ambition at court will prove embarrassing. The ambitions of most of the council rose little higher than a bountiful supply of food and drink and an occasional change of wives. The Prince continued to address unresponsive figures:

'What can we do? These English, and other foreigners, trifle with us. They do not so much as stir to consider our demands. We are treated like children—we, of Ghangistan, whose temples and palaces were weathered when these English hid in caves, whose ancestors reach back unbroken to the creation. We offer them war, and they laugh as one laughs at the ferocity of a cornered mouse. Here we must sit, impotent, while they pour over our country the froth and ferment of their way of life, in mockery of the wisdom of our sacred ancestors.'

Again the Prince paused and looked questioningly about him. At the lack of response he shrugged his shoulders; some of the spirit seemed to go out of him, and he threw out his hands in token of helplessness.

'And we can do nothing. We have no big guns, no aeroplanes. We must sit by and watch our ancient race seduced from its gods, and hear the voice of wisdom drowned by the sounding emptiness of materialism.'

He finished dejectedly. His anger had subsided beneath fatalism, and he brooded amid the respectful, if slightly bored silence of the council. One ancient looked up and studied the Prince. He allowed a decent interval to elapse before he inquired:

'Is it permitted to speak?'

The Prince regarded him with but little lifting of his despondency. 'It is permitted to you, Haramin,' he agreed.

The old man stroked his beard for some moments in placid reflection.

'It has seemed to me,' he began with slow deliberateness, 'that already we are more affected by the Westerners than we acknowledge. Even our methods of thought have become curiously coloured by their mental processes. We begin now to distort our pure wisdom to fit their strange conventions.'

A murmur of protest ran round the council, but none dare give full voice to his indignation, for the old man was privileged.

'Explain the full meaning,' commanded the Prince.

'It is well shown by an example, My Prince. See how these Westerners wage war. First they send a declaration to warn their enemies—is this not absurd? Then they use against that enemy a series of weapons similar to his own—which is plainly ridiculous. They have, in fact, rules for war—a conceit worthy only of children or imbeciles.

'We, in our wisdom, know better. We know that wars should be won or lost; not childishly prolonged until both sides give up for very weakness and weariness. And yet'—he paused and looked around him—'and yet we sit here lamenting our lack of weapons, lamenting that we cannot meet our oppressors on their own ground. It is a foolishness to consider the standards of the West in war.'

The Prince Khordah frowned. The tone of the other's speech displeased him, but he was aware that some deeper thought had prompted it. He asked coldly:

'Is it necessary here, Haramin, to lurk like an old fox in a thicket of words?'

'I have a nephew, Prince, a man of great learning in the ways of the West, yet retaining the wisdom of his ancestors. He has a plan which should interest Your Highness.'

The Prince leaned forward. At last they seemed to be getting somewhere.

'Where is this nephew, Haramin?'

'I have brought him to await Your Highness' summons.'

The Prince struck a silver gong beside him. To the entering servant he said:

'The nephew of Haramin waits. Let him be brought before us.'

CHAPTER ONE

THE MYSTERIOUS GROWTHS

RALPH WAITE's father beamed genially across the dinner-table.

'It's good to have you home again, my boy,' he said. 'How long do you think you can manage?'

Ralph, a lusty, fair-haired young man, turned towards him. 'Only the week-end, I'm afraid, Dad.'

Mrs. Waite looked up with a little wrinkle of concern and disappointment.

'Is that all, dear? Don't you think if you wrote nicely to them they might let you stay a little longer?'

Ralph checked a rising smile. 'I don't think it would be much good writing nicely to Amalgamated Chemicals, Mother,' he said gravely.

'I suppose you know best, dear, but——'

Mr. Waite broke in with some little excitement:

'I've got something to show you after dinner, Ralph. Quite the most remarkable thing in all my gardening experience.'

His eyes were on his plate, so that he missed the look with which his wife favoured him.

'But, dear,' she began, 'Ralph will want to——'

Ralph checked her with a glance. Of course he wanted to go and see Dorothy. His real desire was to rush off at this very moment, but he knew his father's enthusiasm for his hobby. The old man would be sadly disappointed if he could not impress his son with his latest horticultural triumph. After all, Ralph reflected, the old boy got little enough pleasure, pushed away in this little Cornish town for the rest of his life.

'What is it?' he asked.

Mr. Waite chuckled. 'You'll see, my boy. All in good time; all in good time.'

The town of St. Brian lies not far from the south coast of Cornwall. A swift river, the Bod, flows through it on its way to join the English Channel at a point where it is almost the Atlantic Ocean. To the north one can see those strange, dazzling white cones which are the refuse of the clay pits, and from the higher points it is possible to trace the course of the Bod right down to the sea in the south.

The houses are mostly built of grey stone, their roofs clamped down upon them lest they should be whirled off by the gales which in winter sweep in from the Atlantic. In sheltered spots, where they are able to take advantage of kindly climate, flowers and plants thrive, as was excellently testified by Mr. Waite's garden.

Dinner concluded, he led the way importantly across a stretch of smooth lawn to the thick hedge masking the far corner of his ground. As they reached a gap he paused, and with something of the manner of a showman, waved his son forward.

'There, my boy,' he said proudly. 'Just take a look at that!'

Ralph, as he stepped forward to the hedge, was fully prepared to be impressed, but at the sight which met him, the nicely turned phrases he had thought up for the other's gratification fled away. He stared speechlessly for a moment, then:

'What on earth's that?' he demanded.

'Ah, I thought it'd surprise you. Fine growth, what?'

'But—what *is* the thing?' persisted Ralph, gazing in horrified fascination.

'Well,' Mr. Waite admitted doubtfully, 'I don't think it's been named yet—sort of experiment they got me to try out. A new form of marrow or something of the sort, I gather. Wait a minute, and I'll get the letter...'

He bustled across the lawn while his son turned to regard the 'fine growth' with renewed interest. Experiment or not, he decided that it was quite one of the most unwholesome looking plants he had ever seen. Roughly spherical, it reminded him mostly of a pumpkin with a diameter every bit of two feet.

But it was not so much the size which was responsible for his surprise as the colour. It lay before him, clammily glistening in the evening sunlight, a ball of blotchy, virulent yellow. The ground all round it was bare, and it lay on one side attached to the earth only by a poor, twisted wisp of a stalk, as foolishly disproportionate as a pig's tail.

'Must be a good weight, a thing that size,' he muttered to

himself. With some distaste, he inserted his hand beneath it, and then stared at the thing in blank surprise. It weighed possibly a pound.

He was still staring at it when Mr. Waite returned with a paper fluttering in his hand.

'Here you are. That, and the instructions for growing, are all I know about it.'

Ralph took the typewritten letter. It was headed 'Slowitt & Co.,' and underneath in smaller type was added: 'Agents for Experimental Growers' Company.'

Dear Sir [he read], In the course of our experimental work we have succeeded in evolving a new form of vegetable. We have the greatest hopes that this extremely prolific plant will successfully adapt itself to a great range of climatic conditions. In so far as we have been able to reproduce the various conditions in our laboratories, the results leave nothing to be desired, and we now feel that the time has come to put the plant to test in the actual climates it will have to face.

Our agents, in pursuance of our instructions to find persons likely to be interested in this development, forwarded us your name as that of a consistently successful exhibitor at a number of fruit and vegetable shows, and as one who takes an interest in the scientific side of horticulture. We have, therefore, great pleasure in asking you if you would consider assisting us in the introduction of this new form . . .

Ralph read far enough to enable him to grasp essentials.

'This is all very well, Dad,' he remarked. 'But what on earth's the good of the thing? It must be hollow; have you felt its weight?'

'Oh, that's all right. It says in the growing instructions, which they sent with the seeds, that one must not be surprised at the extraordinary lightness. I gather that when it is full-grown it begins to solidify or harden. Though it is a queer looking thing, I'll admit, and so were the seeds.'

He fished in his pocket and found an object which he handed over.

'I kept this one out of curiosity. You see, they've enclosed it—or, rather, several of them—in a kind of capsule. The instructions were emphatic that the capsule must not be opened in any circumstances.'

'Then how——?'

'You just bury the whole thing and water it very plentifully;

I suppose that dissolves the capsule and lets the thing begin to grow. It certainly shows a fine turn of speed. You'd never guess how long it is since I planted this chap.' He stirred the yellow ball with his toe.

Ralph did not attempt the guess. 'How long?' he inquired.

'Three days,' said his father with pride. 'Only three days to reach that size! Of course, I'm not sure how long it will be before it's any use, but it's started very well, and——'

But Mr. Waite's intended lecture was frustrated. His wife's voice tactfully summoned him to the house.

'Don't tell anyone about this, yet, my boy. I promised to keep it quiet till the thing should be full-grown,' he said as he hurried across the lawn.

Ralph thankfully departed on his intended visit. Later, he was unable to remember whether it was curiosity or absence of mind which caused the one remaining seed capsule to find its way into his pocket; he only knew that it was lucky he had kept it.

Dorothy Forbes had expected Ralph earlier. She had even employed sundry of her waiting moments in inventing such reproaches as might be becoming in a lady slightly neglected. It was a pleasant mental exercise, but little more; Ralph's method of greeting did not allow of the interview being placed on a dignified basis.

Instead of venting displeasure, she smoothed her frock, shook back her fair hair, wondered for a moment why one should blush quite so warmly, and suggested that there was a swing seat in the garden.

The swing seat was such a success that it was quite half an hour before an object on the other side of the garden caught Ralph's eye and caused him to sit up, staring. Just visible over the top of a cucumber frame was a curved section of a familiar yellow surface.

'Good Lord!' he said.

'What?' asked Dorothy. Following his line of sight, she added: 'Oh, that's one of Daddy's secrets—you're not supposed to see it.'

'Well, now I have seen it, what about a closer view?'

'I suppose it doesn't really matter, but don't tell him you've seen it.'

A few seconds sufficed to settle any lingering doubt. The plant behind the frame was identical with that in his father's garden, though possibly a few inches smaller.

'That's queer,' Ralph murmured.

Dorothy nodded, though she misapplied the remark.

'I think it's horrid. I told Daddy I'm sure it's unhealthy, but he only laughed at me. Somehow I hate the thing. There's such a nasty, poisonous look about that yellow.'

'He's keeping it secret?'

'Yes; he's very jealous about it. He says it will make him famous one day.'

Ralph nodded. This made it queerer still. He considered for a moment. Two people, each thinking himself unique, were growing this most unprepossessing vegetable.

'What about a little walk?' he suggested. Dorothy, with slight surprise at the sudden change of subject, assented.

It was a wandering stroll, apparently aimless. Nevertheless, it took them close to a number of back gardens. Altogether, they counted over twenty of the strange yellow balls.

CHAPTER TWO

THE RASH

WHEN Ralph returned home to London, it was obvious that in a very short time there would be no more concealment of the strange growths. They were swelling to prodigious sizes with a swiftness which was rendering secrecy impossible. Already two peppery gentlemen who had considered themselves favoured experimenters had discovered one another's rivalry and were indulging in wordy unpleasantness.

It could not be long before all twenty, and other yet undiscovered growers, would hear about it and join in the indignation. Dorothy's next letter, therefore, did not astonish him when it announced that the cats were out of the bag and the gardeners of the town of St. Brian were in full cry for one another's blood.

'When our fathers discovered that they were rivals,' she wrote, 'it was bad enough. But now there are more than a score of them tearing their hair and threatening legal proceedings. It isn't only in St. Brian, either. We've heard reports that hundreds of gardeners both in Cornwall and west Devon are growing the things.

'Ours is so big, too. It's over four feet in diameter now, and looks more evil than ever. I'm beginning to feel a bit afraid of it; I know that sounds silly, but it's the truth. I told Daddy the other day that there was something wicked about it and that I was sure it was never meant to grow in England, but he only laughed and said neither were potatoes. All the same, I think the balls are beastly things. I hear that some boys cut the stalk of one near Newquay and rolled it down the cliffs so that it burst. I'd like to do the same with ours, only I hate the idea of touching the thing—ugh!'

The earlier part of the letter caused Ralph some quiet smiles. He knew very well the temperament of the amateur gardener, with all its jealousies and enthusiasms, and the prospect of the warfare which must now be disturbing the community could give the unprejudiced onlooker no little amusement. But he grew more serious as he recalled the sickening appearance of those growths when they were only two feet in diameter; already they had swelled to four....

Unreasoning as Dorothy's dislike of them might be, he found himself able to understand it and to sympathise with it. He was worried by the feeling, for he preferred reason to prejudice.

Nevertheless the matter was gradually slipping into the back of his mind until it was recalled a few days later by a paragraph tucked away at the foot of a newspaper column:

'Several cases are reported from Newquay, the well-known Cornish holiday resort, of an outbreak of rash which is puzzling the local doctors. It is thought that the condition may be consequent upon prolonged or injudicious exposure of the skin while sunbathing.'

For a moment he was puzzled to know when he had lately thought of Newquay; then he remembered that it was near there that the yellow ball had been pushed over the cliffs.

Dorothy's next letter informed him that a state of excitement was prevailing all over the West Country. The inhabitants, it appeared, had split into two schools of thought on the subject of the yellow balls.

The growers and their friends were noisily upholding their rights to grow what they liked on their own land, while the opposition, without apparent grounds for the statement, proclaimed that the things were unhealthy. They shared, Dorothy surmised, her revulsion against them. Some days before a minor riot of protest had taken place in Bodmin. In the course of it, three balls had been slashed open.

After he had finished the letter, Ralph turned to his newspaper and found information which brought wrinkles of speculation to his forehead.

The cases of rash at Newquay had become serious. One of the victims had died, and the others were in a precarious condition. It was, according to the correspondent, impossible to state definitely that the rash was the cause of death, but he evidently had more than suspicions.

Then followed the information that the same mysterious rash had made its appearance at Bodmin, coupled with an assurance that it could not, in the later cases, be in any way attributed to sunbathing.

Thoughtfully, Ralph withdrew his father's seed capsule from his pocket and regarded it.

'I may be a fool. It's probably just a coincidence, but it's worth investigating.' he told himself.

Before he sought his own office, he called in at the laboratory of a friend who worked in the bio-chemical department of Amalgamated Chemicals, Ltd.

Two days passed before he heard any result of the examination of the capsule. Then Arnold Jordan, the bio-chemist, entered his office just as he was finishing off for the day.

'You've tackled it?' asked Ralph.

Arnold nodded.

'Yes, I've tackled it. And I'm not sure whether I owe you a dinner for putting me on to it, or whether you owe me a dinner for putting in the devil of a lot of work. On the whole, I approve of the latter.'

'Oh, all right. You look as if some good food wouldn't do you any harm. Come on!'

It was not until the end of the dinner, over the coffee and cigarettes, that Arnold consented to discuss his conclusions. Then he began with an expostulation.

'I do think, old man, you might have given me a bit more warning about that beastly stuff you brought along.'

'Well, I told you I had an idea it was pretty noxious,' Ralph pointed out. 'But, after all, the reason I brought it at all was that I didn't know much about it.'

'Where did you get it?' asked Arnold curiously.

His manner shed its slight banter, and a look of seriousness crept into his eyes, as Ralph explained.

'Good God! You don't mean to say these things are being grown! What for?'

'Food—what else does one grow vegetables for?'

'But this is a fungus.'

'I thought it looked that way, but quite a lot of fungi are edible when they're cooked.'

Arnold failed to reply for some seconds; he seemed not to have heard and was staring fixedly into space. When he turned back Ralph was startled by the expression on his face.

'Do you know anything about fungi?'

'No,' replied Ralph promptly.

'Well, I'll be short about it, but I'll try to show you what this business means. First of all, there are two types of fungi. Either a fungus is a saprophyte and lives upon decaying matter, or else it is a parasite, in which case it exists upon living matter. As far as the saprophytes are concerned—well, you've eaten a good many in your time as mushrooms or cheese, or a hundred other ways; but the parasites are not so numerous—the kind which most frequently afflicts human beings is ringworm.

'Now this particular bit of evil which you kindly handed to me is neither one nor other of these forms; it is both. That is to say that it flourishes equally well on decay, or on living flesh. Do you see what I'm getting at?'

Ralph began to see.

'This thing,' Arnold continued, 'is not only a parasite, but a more vicious parasite than any known. All these growths you have told me of must be scotched—utterly wiped out and obliterated before they can become ripe. Once allowed to burst and scatter their spores——' He spread his hands expressively.

Ralph regarded him nervously. 'You're sure of this?'

Arnold nodded. 'Of the danger I am certain. About the plant itself I'm very puzzled. Obviously the spores were enclosed in a soluble capsule so that they might be planted and brought to fruit in safety.

'If your information is correct, the whole thing seems to be deliberate, and on a large scale. It is not merely a case of scattering a few spores to grow haphazard, but immense trouble has been taken to induce people to cultivate the fungi so that millions of spores will be spread.'

He paused, and added: 'It's up to us to try to stop this thing, old man. Somebody must, or it's God help thousands of miserable people!'

Ralph was silent. He remembered the mysterious rash at Newquay, and the similar outbreak at Bodmin. He recalled, too, the sight of that slimy, yellow ball in his father's garden, and his face was pale as he looked at the other.

'We're too late,' he said. 'It's begun.'

CHAPTER THREE

THE DANGER INCREASES

'STUFF!' said Major Forbes, with some violence. 'Stuff and nonsense! You ought to have known better, young man, than to come to me with an old wive's tale like that.'

Ralph gave up his attempt to convince the old man. After Arnold's warning of the previous evening, he had caught the earliest possible train for the West Country and travelled all night. There had not been any time to lose. So far as he knew, the enormous puffballs might burst of their own accord at any hour, quite apart from the danger of one of them receiving an accidental puncture and spreading its spores about the neighbourhood.

He had arrived, tired and anxious, to be greeted by both his own and Dorothy's father with complete disbelief. In vain he put the cases of rash forward as evidence and quoted Arnold's warning. It was useless. Each, at the back of his mind, seemed determined that this was some deep ruse by rival growers to get him out of the way; and, even if the thing was a fungus, what man worth his salt was going to be scared by a mere puffball, however big?

'No,' Major Forbes repeated firmly. 'You say that your mother and my daughter are willing to leave—of course they are. Women are always wanting to run up to London for some fal-lal or other. Take 'em along with you; the change'll do 'em good. But don't come bothering me!'

And there was a similar interview with his own father. Mrs. Waite attempted to smooth over her husband's irritation.

'Now, don't worry your father any more, dear. You must see that he doesn't want to come. I should like to go to London for a week or so, but don't bother him. I should have to go soon, in any case, to do a little shopping.'

'But you don't understand, Mother. This is really serious— it's dangerous. These things he is growing are rank poison!'

Mrs. Waite looked a little distressed.

'Do you really think so, dear? I mean, it seems so unlikely— and the people who sent them don't seem to think so. They definitely said they were vegetables.'

'Never mind what they said. Take it from me—or, rather, from Arnold, who is an expert—that these things are deadly and must be destroyed.'

'Eh? What's that?' Mr. Waite chimed in. 'Destroyed? I'd like

to see anyone attempt to destroy my specimen. I'd show him
what's what! There's still a law in the land.'

'You'll promise me, won't you, John, not to eat any of it
while I am away?' Mrs. Waite spoke as though her presence
should nullify the plant's poisonous quality. Her husband un-
graciously conceded the point.

'All right,' he said gruffly. 'I'll promise you that much—
though I repeat that I think the whole thing is a scare.'

'Well, if you won't come, I can't make you,' said Ralph, 'but
I do beg of you——'

Again he went over the details of Arnold's warning, only to
succeed in thinning his father's temper and his own. At last he
turned back to Mrs. Waite.

'This is a waste of time. You'd better pack your things and
get ready, Mother.'

'You mean now, dear?'

'Yes. At once.'

'Oh, but I couldn't possibly be ready before tomorrow.
There are such a lot of things which just have to be finished
off.'

Ralph went around again to see Dorothy.

'We'll have to wait until tomorrow,' he told her. 'I can't
make them believe there's any danger in delay.'

'Well, one day won't make much difference,' she suggested.

'It might. I want to get you both out of here as soon as
possible. Any moment it may be too late.'

'We'll be right away this time tomorrow. Now let's talk
about something else.'

'I can't think of anything else. I've heard Arnold on the
subject, and you haven't. Let's go out and have a look at the
brutes.'

'Hullo,' said Arnold, entering Ralph's office. 'Where the devil
have you been for the last two days?'

'Down in Cornwall; trying to make my people clear out.'

'Did you?'

'Got Dorothy and my mother up here. Neither of the fathers
would shift—stubborn old fools! What have you been up to?'

Arnold disregarded the question. 'You've done all you
could?'

'Of course I have—short of kidnapping the old blighters.'

Arnold looked grave.

'I'm afraid the news is rather serious,' he began. 'The morning after our chat I went round to see a fellow I know at the
Ministry of Health, and they welcomed me there with open

arms. This thing is a good many times bigger than we thought it was. The authorities have been minimising—didn't want to ruin the holiday traffic, or some rot like that. They told me that there have been hundreds of cases of the rash and several dozen deaths. Not only that, but soon after the dead have been buried those yellow puff-balls start growing from the graves.

'Their experts were as sure as I was that this form of fungus has never been heard of before, and most of us are pretty certain that somebody has been up to some rather ugly cross-breeding, with malice aforethought. They issued orders yesterday that no more of the things were to be planted, but that was useless; already round the centres where the things have burst, the place is littered with the balls.'

'Growing already?'

'Thousands of them, around Newquay and Bodmin and several other places. And nobody dare touch them.'

'But aren't they doing anything—destroying them?'

'How?'

'Can't they—can't they spray them with acids, or something? Do you realise that the first lot hasn't reached its natural bursting point yet? All this second crop is the result of accidental breakage. God knows what will happen if they are allowed to burst.'

'Nobody seems to know how to tackle the situation. But they're not lying down; they see the danger all right, and they're going after it day and night. You can see yourself that the problem is how to destroy the balls without liberating the spores.'

'There must be some way...'

'Oh, they'll find a way, but it's got to be drastic and well organised. The thing they're most anxious about at present is that there shall be no panic. You know what people are like when they lose their heads. If they go wild and start smashing the things wholesale, there'll be hell to pay. You can take it from me that the departments concerned are already making things hum behind the scenes.'

'Meanwhile, the first crop of balls must be pretty nearly ripe...'

Ralph searched the lounge of the hotel where his mother and Dorothy were staying. He eventually found Mrs. Waite occupying a comfortable arm-chair in a secluded corner. He greeted her, and seated himself beside her.

'Where's Dorothy?' he asked a few minutes later. 'Getting ready?'

'Ready?' repeated Mrs. Waite inquiringly.

'We arranged to go out and dance this evening.'

'Oh, dear me, of course. Then you didn't hear from her—she said she would telephone.'

'She didn't. What was it about?'

'Well, she won't be able to go out tonight. You see, she's gone down to Cornwall.'

'She's what?' shouted Ralph, in a voice which echoed across the lounge.

'Yes, dear, she said she felt she must go to Cornwall,' Mrs. Waite repeated placidly.

'But why didn't you stop her? Surely you realise the danger? Good God, she may have caught the rash—she may die of it!'

Mrs. Waite looked a little shocked.

'Well, dear, I did tell her that I didn't think you would like it. But she seemed so anxious about her father—such a nice trait in a young girl, I always think—that I didn't feel it was right to interfere.'

Ralph made no reply. His mother, glancing at him, saw that his face was drawn into tight creases. There was an expression in his eyes which hurt her. For the first time she began to appreciate that there was real fear behind his actions and talk of the last few days. Futilely she started to talk when she should have kept silent.

'Of course, this may not be so very dangerous after all. I expect it's just another of these scares. Things will be all right in the end, and we shall all have a good laugh at our fears. Don't you worry, dear; I expect—good gracious!'

Ralph was roused out of his thoughts to see what had caused her exclamation of surprise. He looked up to find himself facing his father and Major Forbes. An hour ago he would have been pleased to see them and cheered by the thought that the whole party was reunited; but now his greeting was cold.

Major Forbes looked around him.

'And where is Dorothy?' he asked.

Ralph answered him bitterly.

'She's gone to save you,' he said.

CHAPTER FOUR

FIGHTING THE MENACE

'YES, my boy,' said Mr. Waite, 'we certainly owe our escape to you. You seemed so positive about the danger that I did a bit of investigating; poked about a bit among the local officials.

'It was old Inspector Roberts who gave me the tip—he's always considered himself in my debt over that matter of his boy. "Mr. Waite," he said, "I ought not to tell you; in fact, I'm breaking orders by doing so, but if you take my advice you'll get out of the district just as soon as you can." '

'Yes, it was a straight tip, by gad!' agreed the Major. 'I managed to hear a few things about the country round about —pretty bad. Some fool started a panic in Launceston. Half the town was out with sticks and stones and knives, smashing all the yellow balls they could find.

'A man told me the ground was white with spores, as if there had been a snowstorm. Some of the growers tried to interfere, and there was something like a battle. Pretty much the same thing seems to have happened in Tavistock and other places in west Devon.'

Ralph looked up.

'Spores or riots,' he said, 'I'm going down by the midnight train to get Dorothy out of that. What's the time now?'

The Major snorted,

'Don't be a fool, young man! The girl's all right. She'll be back any moment now, I'll warrant. They're not allowing anyone to enter the area now, so she'll *have* to come back. Your father and I came out on one of the last trains allowed through.'

'What's the time?' Ralph demanded again.

'Twenty to ten,' said the Major, 'and I repeat that you are wasting your time if you go down there.'

'The news,' Mr. Waite said suddenly. 'There's sure to be something about all this.' He called a waiter and asked for the radio to be switched on. A few moments later they were listening to the calm, familiar voice of the London announcer.

The general weather report was unencouraging and the voice went on to add:

'Gale warning. The Meteorological Office issued the following warning to shipping at twenty hours, Greenwich Mean Time. Strong westerly winds, rising to gale force, may be expected on all the Irish coast. English coast west of a line from

Southampton to Newcastle, and English Channel.'

Ralph glanced at his father, who caught his eye, but sent a warning glance in the direction of his mother. Both of them grasped the implication. Thousands of light, yellow balls attached merely by skimpy stalks—and a gale rising. . . .

The announcer began on the news:

'We are asked by the Ministry of Transport to broadcast the following. Suspension of service. All train services between Exeter and points west thereof have been temporarily suspended. Further details will be announced tomorrow.'

The Major looked at Ralph triumphantly.

'I told you so! They're isolating the whole district. There's no point in your going down. We shall have Dorothy back here in no time.'

But Ralph was unconvinced. Dorothy had set out to get to her home, and he had a horrid fear that she would do it if it were humanly possible. The Major did not seem to know his own daughter's tenacity of purpose. Ralph stood up with determination.

'I'm going down there *now*. There are still cars, even if they have stopped the trains.'

Thump . . . thump . . . thump . . . went Ralph's mallet. It was three days since he had left London, and now he was engaged in driving stakes into the hard soil of Dartmoor.

A message earlier in the day had informed him that no news had been received of Dorothy. There could be no doubt that she had been trapped in the isolated area and was now—if she had succeeded in reaching St. Brian—still forty or fifty miles to the west of him. He reflected angrily on the events which had landed him at his present occupation.

He had rushed from the hotel in search of Arnold. Before midnight he had borrowed the other's car and was running down Piccadilly, in company with the taxis of homeward-bound theatre-goers. The traffic grew faster and sparser as he passed through sprawling suburbs. He looked forward to showing a good turn of speed on the Great West Road. But when he reached it the volume of traffic had undeniably increased once more.

Long lines of trucks, not too punctilious about keeping to the side of the road, stretched before him. A constant flow of private cars against him, unprecedented for the time of night, made it a difficult business to overtake the trucks. Ralph cursed the obstruction of the lumbering line and noticed for the first time that they were not commercial vans, but were painted khaki or grey, with Army markings on their sides. He swore again. A piece of foul luck to get mixed up in Army manoeuvres; but perhaps they would drop off at Aldershot. They did not. They held on the road to the west and, to his exasperation, were augmented by hundreds more.

'Anybody would think,' he muttered to himself, 'that there was a war on. The whole blooming Army seems to be going my way!'

To add to his troubles, the wind was rising, bringing with it sharp flurries of rain. Instead of making a dash through the night as he had intended, his speed was reduced to a crawl. Only infrequently did the traffic against him allow him to cut past a few of the lumbering shapes ahead. It was full daylight long before he reached Exeter, and he passed through the narrow streets of the old city still escorted by the Army wagons.

Two miles beyond, the road was blocked by a barricade. Sentries with fixed bayonets were assisting the police to turn back all private cars. The representatives of both forces were equally unmoved by his offers of money or his loss of temper.

'It's no good makin' a fuss, young feller,' advised a police sergeant. 'If I'd been taking money today, I could have made my fortune and retired on it. You get back 'ome now!'

There had been nothing for it but to turn his car round and drive sullenly back to Exeter. There he munched a necessary, though unappreciated, meal, while he decided on the next move.

'No private cars along 'ere,' the policeman had said. But the trucks were going through—those same damned trucks which had hindered him all night. Hundreds of them. They were passed without question, and, moreover, without a search. It ought to be possible to jump one and stow away. . . .

After a number of uncomfortable miles the truck stopped. The tail-board was lowered.

' 'Ere, you, come along out of it,' demanded a voice. A hand fastened firmly on to Ralph's collar and dragged him painfully from his hiding-place amid wooden stakes and rolls of barbed wire. He landed among a group of men under the command of a sergeant. The latter came close to him, his pointed moustaches adding ferocity to his expression as he shouted:

'What the —— blazes do you think you were doing in that —— lorry? You come along 'ere with me.'

The officer to whom he was taken had heard him out and then regarded him seriously.

'I like your spirit,' he said, 'but just listen to me a minute.

You seem to know something of the situation, but you're tackling it the wrong way. It's no good your going over there.' He waved his hand to the west. 'You couldn't do a damned thing if you got through, except make yourself another victim.

'Your girl doesn't want you to die. You know, if you give it a moment's thought, that she'd be far prouder of you for helping to fight this stuff and beat it; for helping to blot the damned growths out and make thousands of people safe.'

'But she's——!'

'And don't you realise that from the body of every man who dies out there, more of the yellow balls grow? If you go out there, you'll not only be helpless, but you'll be giving your body to feed them. No, my lad, your job is to help us to fight against the menace. This is a state of emergency, and we need all the help we can get. What about it?'

Ralph at length consented, though with not too good a grace. He knew the officer was right. It was his job to fight, not to throw away his life, but ... He did not quite trust himself. Sometime the urge to find Dorothy might prove too strong for him. . . .

His working partner's voice broke in on his thoughts. 'What d'yer say to a cigarette, mate?'

Ralph delivered a final blow to the stake they were fixing, and agreed. To right and left of them across the moorland hills stretched the long line of posts. Here and there, parties of men who had completed their sections were already beginning to weave an impenetrable net of barbed wire around the stakes. Behind, on the roadway, was a never-ending line of trucks loaded with more wire and yet more stakes, while closer, between themselves and the road, a sweating army of men laboured to dig a broad trench.

Ralph was amazed at the organisation which in two or three days had enabled the authorities to be well on the way to barricading off a whole corner of the country. At the same time he was puzzled; the purpose of the wire was obvious, but he failed to understand the reason for the broad, shallow trench. Nor was his partner, Bill 'Awkins, as he called himself, able to explain its use. But he was ready to concede that the authorities knew what they were about, and were not wasting any time.

'Yus,' he remarked, 'they're quick on the job, they are. Why, a few nights ago there was a gale warning—p'raps you 'eard it?'

Ralph nodded.

'Well, the minute they knew that, they changed their plans

like a flash. This 'ere line was to 'ave been miles farther forward; they'd even begun to get the supplies up there when the order for retreat came. You see, the wind in these parts is pretty near always from the west; that's what's got 'em scared —the idea of this stuff being swept right across the country. If it's true what they say about some feller a-startin' it on purpose, then 'e picked a likely place.

' 'Owever, the wind didn't come to much, after all. Most of them yeller balls just rolled a bit, and then got stuck in the valleys and 'ollows and suchlike—blamed lucky it was, too.'

'Then all this,' said Ralph, indicating the defences, 'is in case a real storm comes along?'

'That'll be about the idea,' Bill agreed.

They smoked for a while in silence. From time to time a great plane would roar across the moor, carrying food supplies to be dropped to the isolated; and, once, a large caterpillar tractor came swaying and plunging past them, bound for the west. Bill grinned as he caught sight of the men aboard it and the instruments they held.

'What are they?' asked Ralph. 'Looks like a squad of divers going on duty.'

'Asbestos suits and masks,' the other explained. 'And they're carrying flame-throwers. Those'll give the blinkin' things a bit of a toasting!'

CHAPTER FIVE

THE ATTACK ON THE WIND

SOME six nights later, Ralph sat with a group in the stable which was their billet. One man was holding forth pessimistically.

'I suppose they're doing a bit of good with all this flame-throwing and whatnot, but it ain't getting 'em far. It's the plant underneath that they want to get at, not just the yellow balls. They're only the fruit—you don't kill an apple-tree by knocking off the apples. Fungi have a sort of web of stuff spreading all through the ground around them; that's the life of the things, and that's what they——'

There came a thunderous knocking on the door and a stentorian call to turn out.

'Wind's rising,' said the sergeant. 'You all know your jobs. Get to 'em, and look slippy!'

The wind swept in from the Atlantic at gale force. The first few puffs stirred the yellow balls and rolled them a little at the ends of their skimpy stalks. Later followed a gust which twisted them so that the stalks snapped and they were free to roll where the wind urged. As the pressure grew to a steady blast, it swept up a mass of the light balls and carried them bounding across the countryside, an army of vegetable invaders launching their attack to capture the land and destroy human beings.

The wind of a week before had moved only the balls in the most exposed positions, but this time, none but the youngest and least developed had the strength in their stalks to resist the air which tore at them. Every now and then a splashing flurry of white would spring from the hurtling, bouncing horde as the tough, yellow skin of one was ripped by some sharp spike or the corner of a roof. Then the great spores themselves were caught up by the wind and carried on faster as an advance guard of the yellow army.

The gale seemed to display a diabolical zest for this new game. It increased its force to drive the balls yet more furiously. Hedges, ditches and trees failed to check the headlong charge. Even rivers proved no obstacle; with the wind behind, the balls sailed across in their thousands, bobbing and jerking on the rough surface.

They were thrust relentlessly down the narrow streets of the little towns, jostling and jamming against the corners of the buildings until the houses were hidden in a cloud of swirling spores, and the surviving balls tore loose to follow bowling in the wake of their fellows.

This time, the wind did not desert them. Many lodged in sheltered hollows, but they served merely to fill them up and make a path over which the rest could travel. The wave of invaders climbed the slopes and swept up and out on to the moor, where, unobstructed, they gathered speed to charge yet more swiftly upon the defenders.

There was a line of fire across the country. Ralph had soon learned the purpose of the broad trench. Filled now with blazing oil and wood, it formed a rampart of flame.

'Here they come,' cried the look-out, clinging to a swaying perch high above.

Soon all could see the few whirling balls which seemed to lead the way, and the turgid mass of yellow pressing close behind the outrunners.

They held their breaths. . . .

The first balls hurled themselves to destruction upon a

cheval-de-frise, a hedge of bristling spikes which slit and tore their skins and set free the spores to go scudding on into the flames. But they came too thick and fast. In many places they piled up solid against the sharp fence, forming ramps for those behind to come racing over the top and fall among the meshes of barbed wire.

Every now and then a ball seemed to leap as though it possessed motive power within itself. Missing the wire, it would bowl across no-man's-land to a final explosion in the flaming ditch, its burning spores shooting aloft like the discharge of a monstrous firework.

'My God!' muttered the man next to Ralph. 'If this wind doesn't drop soon, we'll be done. Look at that!'

'That' was one of several balls which, miraculously escaping all traps prepared for it, had leaped past them into the darkness behind.

'They'll catch it in the nets back there and burn it when the wind drops,' Ralph replied with a confidence which he scarcely felt. 'The thing that worries me is that the fires may die down—we can't get near to fuel them from the lee side here.'

But, as luck had it, the fires outlasted the wind.

'Men,' began the officer in charge, the next morning, 'it was a pretty near thing last night, and we have to thank providence that we successfully withstood it. But we can't afford to waste time. We've got to get to work at once. There may be another wind any time, and that mass of stuff choking the spikes must be cleared before it comes. I want every man who has experience of flame-throwers to step forward.'

Ralph, in company with many others, stepped out. He had no knowledge of flame-throwers, but it was the only way he could acquire an asbestos suit and get out into the danger area. For more than a week he had stifled his anxiety to know Dorothy's fate, and now he could bear it no longer.

As he struggled into the heavy covering which would not only insulate him from fire, but also withstand the deadly spores, he turned over his plan. Perhaps such a simple getaway was unworthy of the name of a plan. Roughly, it consisted in placing himself among the foremost of those who would be clearing the ground with their fire-sprays, and working gradually ahead until the thickly scattered balls should give him concealment from the rest of the party. All he had to do then was to walk off to the west.

The only risk, once he was away, was that one of the food-carrying planes might spot him. But the chance was remote, and it was unlikely that a lone straggler would be considered worthy of investigation.

The scheme worked as he had expected. No hue and cry was raised after him as he wormed away. In a very little while he stood alone at the threshold of the stricken district.

As far as he could see in three directions, the land was dotted with the yellow balls, poised ominously where the wind had left them, and seeming to wait for the next gale to pick them up and send them swirling onward to more victims. Surrounded by the evilly glittering skins, he shuddered for a moment before his determination reasserted itself.

He drew a deep breath through his mask, threw back his head and strode on, a lone, grey figure, the only moving object in a scene of desolation.

In the first village he found a motor-cycle with its tank half-full, and for six miles it shattered the silence of the moor as he drove it, zigzagging to avoid the growths which littered the road. Then came a sharp valley so choked with balls that he must leave the motor-cycle, throw away the heavy flame-thrower and climb across the balls themselves.

On several occasions one burst beneath his weight and he dropped some feet in a flurry of spores which threatened to choke his breathing mask until he could wipe them away. Then, laboriously, he must pick himself up and struggle on, while streams of sweat soaked his clothing beneath the clumsy suit. Once he almost turned back to pick up the flame-thrower with the idea of burning his way through the mass, but he remembered that its cylinder was already half discharged. Desperately he battled, until at last his feet found the bracken and heather of the farther hill-side.

Afterwards, he could recall little of that journey. He became uncertain even of the number of days which passed as he tramped on and scrambled through one choked valley after another.

Only odd incidents startled him now and then out of a stupid weariness : the little town on the moor where men and women lay dead in the streets while the fungus preyed on them, and the windows of the houses were full of yellow balls which mercifully hid the rooms .. the voice of a madman chanting hymns in a barricaded hut; hymns which turned to cursing blasphemies as he heard Ralph's step outside ... the things which had been men, and which he was forced to move when thirst tortured him to find a drink in a dead inn. . . .

But somehow, with dulled senses, he strove on through the nightmare while with every mile he covered, the fear of what he might find at his goal increased.

He felt that he was almost home when he crossed the River Tamar which separates Devon from Cornwall. The bridge was choked with the fungus. Upstream was wedged a solid mass of yellow, but below it the river raced, bearing an occasional serenely floating ball which would later meet its fate before the fire boats in Plymouth Sound.

At last, St. Brian. The balls were fewer here. The wind had carried most of them away. His own home. Farther on, Dorothy's home—blank, locked . . . deserted?

He broke a window to enter, and wandered about the empty rooms. No trace of fungus inside the house. No trace, either, of Dorothy. Perhaps she was upstairs. He was weak and hungry. Every step of the climb was an effort.

At the door of her room he hesitated. Would she be there; the yellow balls growing from her, feeding upon her still body? He opened the door; anything was better now than uncertainty. No one on the bed—no one in the room at all. He began to laugh hysterically. Dorothy had fooled the balls. They hadn't got her. She was alive, he was sure now—alive in spite of those damned balls. He fell on the bed, half-laughing, half-crying.

Suddenly he stopped. A sound outside. Voices? Painfully he crawled across to look out of the window. A group of people was coming up the road. People he knew. They were wearing ordinary clothes, and among them was Dorothy—Dorothy!

He tore off his mask and tried to shout to them. Funny; his voice wouldn't work, somehow. Never mind. Dorothy had fooled the yellow balls. That was damned funny. He was laughing again as he sank to the floor.

'Yes, dear, I'm real,' said Dorothy, at the bedside.

'But—but how——?'

'When I got here I found that Daddy had gone. The only thing was for me to go, too. Several of us went down the river in a boat and rowed along nearly to Land's End. Right in the toe of Cornwall we were beyond the balls, and to windward of them. Then, when it was safe——'

'Safe?'

'Yes, dear. It's safe now. The balls are just like an ordinary fungus now—they don't attack living things any more. Then we came home and found you here.'

'But——'

'Not now. You mustn't talk any more, dear. You've been very ill, you know.'

Ralph acquiesced. He went to sleep peacefully, her hand in his and a smile on his face.

ENVOI

THE Prince Khordah of Ghangistan regarded the nephew of Haramin, bent low before him.

'Your plan has failed,' he said.

The nephew of Haramin nodded dumbly.

'But,' continued the Prince, 'it has cost that accursed country more than did ever our wars—and we have lost nothing. Tell me, why did it fail?'

'Your Highness, the stock did not breed true. After two or so generations it was no longer a parasite, but had reverted to a common, saprophytic fungus.'

'Which, however, it will take them many years to suppress?'

'Many years,' the other repeated hopefully.

The Prince Khordah spent a few moments in contemplation.

'We are not displeased,' he said at length. 'Doubtless the first arrow did not kill a lion. There are other means, nephew of Haramin?'

The bent figure heaved a sigh of relief.

'There are other means,' he agreed.